Advance Praise for

Walking on Cowrie Shells

"*Walking on Cowrie Shells* is a virtuosic, kaleidoscopic debut, one that rejects the paint-by-number templates of storytelling to refresh our sense of what fiction can be and do. Nana Nkweti's supersonic prose breaks the sound barrier as she crisscrosses genres and cultures and continents, from a zombie outbreak in Cameroon to a *künstler-roman* set at Comic-Con. Satirical, playful, keenly critical of the racist stereotypes and received narratives that limit women's lives, these polyphonic tales are a joy to read. Nkweti's ambitious, amphibious tales capture the diverse and complex experience of 'hyphenated Americans' who, like Nkweti, have deep roots in Africa and America. It would be impossible to overstate how much I love this book, and its author."　　　**—Karen Russell, author of** *Orange World*

"Nana Nkweti's exuberant collection is full of stories that weave together love and friendship, horror and comedy, all with great deftness. The characters, straddling continents and cultures, carving out a place for themselves, remind me of home. A wonderful debut."
　　—Yaa Gyasi, author of *Transcendent Kingdom* **and** *Homegoing*

"These genre-leaping stories are funny and heartbreaking and wonderfully ferocious; it's been ages since I've read sentences with this much verve and snap. *Walking on Cowrie Shells* is a delightful, rollicking debut."   —**Carmen Maria Machado, author of *Her Body and Other Parties* and *In the Dream House***

"Let us thank whoever granted Nana Nkweti her all-access pass to the human soul, for with it she is able to gain entry into the lives of women and men, children and adults, the damaged and the damaging, the human and the not-quite, all with equal clarity and conviction. *Walking on Cowrie* Shells is a collection of verve, audacity, and consummate control. That it is her first book makes it all the more astonishing."   —**Kevin Brockmeier, author of *The Ghost Variations***

"Nana Nkweti trills and enchants. This totally vibrant collection spins a wonder of love and horror. Each fresh universe is more captivating than the next. Always human, *Walking on Cowrie Shells* searches through the real and into the hyperreal. Nkweti's words are dazzlingly energetic, world-ranging and straight-up brilliant."
          —**Samantha Hunt, author of *The Dark Dark***

Walking on Cowrie Shells

Walking on Cowrie Shells

Stories

Nana Nkweti

Graywolf Press

Stories in this collection originally appeared in different form in the following publications:

"Rain Check at MomoCon" as "Marginalia" in *Hunger Mountain*

"The Devil Is a Liar" in the *Masters Review*

"It Takes a Village Some Say" in the *Baffler*

"It Just Kills You Inside" in *New Orleans Review*

"Schoolyard Cannibal" in *Brittle Paper*

"Dance the *Fiya* Dance" as "My Own Flesh and Blood" in *Killens Review of Arts & Letters*

This publication is made possible, in part, by the voters of Minnesota through a Minnesota State Arts Board Operating Support grant, thanks to a legislative appropriation from the arts and cultural heritage fund. Significant support has also been provided by Target Foundation, the McKnight Foundation, the Lannan Foundation, the Amazon Literary Partnership, and other generous contributions from foundations, corporations, and individuals. To these organizations and individuals we offer our heartfelt thanks.

MINNESOTA
STATE ARTS BOARD

CLEAN
WATER
LAND &
LEGACY
AMENDMENT

Published by Graywolf Press
250 Third Avenue North, Suite 600
Minneapolis, Minnesota 55401

www.graywolfpress.org

Published in the United States of America

ISBN 978-1-64445-054-3

2 4 6 8 9 7 5 3 1
First Graywolf Printing, 2021

Library of Congress Control Number: 2020944193

Cover design: Walter Green

Dedicated to

my dad, Dr. David Atehfor Nkweti, thank you for "tchingalinga" and all the harmony-filled folklore you shared and for home libraries chockful of *Nat Geo*s and encyclopedias that gave me the world. And to my mumsy and bona fide shero, Dr. Christina Nana Nkweti, for choosing joy each day and placing childhood-me in every enrichment program—from flute to ballet—so I could be my best self.

Contents

Walking on Cowrie Shells

It Takes a Village Some Say

Volume I: Our Girl

I

Don't believe everything you read in the tabloids. We're nothing like the others. We're not *the Slick Salikis* splashed page to page in the papers; a couple so utterly obsessed with living the good life, so concerned with keeping up appearances that we pimped out our own daughter. Fabrications. Rag sheet revisionist history. All of it. We did our best by Our Girl.

She was eleven years old when we got her, Our Girl. She came to us with a shocking expedited-shipping efficiency, after years of adoption delays: endless home studies, background checks, credit checks, health checks—then *ding-dong, ding-dong*, a child, handily home-delivered. Imported from the motherland. She was bundled up in this sad little polyester coat, the color of off-brand cola—fudgy-brown, tasteless, fizzy—utterly useless in warding off the cold and bluster of that winter night. We pulled her shivering frame into the warmth of our home and she scuttled off to an entryway corner—so straight-backed and vigilant between our coatrack and umbrella stand.

Her guardian, Mrs. Ndukong, a booming storm cloud of a woman, thundered in behind her. Teeth chattering. Chatter chattering: *Hello, hello! It's so cold, so cold.* They had just been to Houston she told us (*so warm!*) and then on to (*so windy!*) Chicago. She pronounced the latter "Qi-cargo," sounding vaguely reminiscent of some new age travelware boutique, a *nag champa*–scented place specializing in vegan carry-ons for the ashram hermitage set. It was the kind of shop we might have frequented in our East Village heydays; before our vacation fund became the baby fund, before we moved out of the city to a home with a backyard and a swing set and a better school system for our someday children.

"The girl? Call her anything, anything you like," she said. "Call me Aunty Gladys. 'Mrs. Ndukong.' Hmph. So formal, so formal. We are good friends now, *no so?*" Her bobble-headed yes preemptively settled the matter to her liking.

We were seated in the formal living room. We could see that Aunty Gladys was impressed. She was meant to be. It was our showcase parlor: chandeliered, marbled, credenzaed; a place where we received guests with a dazzling solicitousness typically the dominion of ambassadors feting visiting state dignitaries. Our Girl sat mutely by the flames of our hearth while we beamed at her from the comfy remove of a Chesterfield sofa.

"Mrs. Du . . ." we began, our eyes locked on each other, before we turned, opening up to our newfound "good friend." "*Aunty Gladys,* you have no idea how long we've been waiting for this. We're just so grateful—"

"Nonsense, nonsense. It is the girl's family that should be grateful," she answered. "Grateful that one of you is from Cameroon so she will know her culture. Not grow up like these young girls twerking their *makande* on television. Godless Americ—" she stopped to gape silently at the salt and pepper set we made sitting there "—sorry, sorry. The cold has scattered my brains."

We were suitably understanding. How could we be otherwise? What followed was all courtesy and business: *Yes, Our Girl had all the appropriate papers. The girl's parents? Her father, may he rest, would be so honored by this opportunity for his youngest daughter to live in white man country. Her mother? Back home, with six younger sisters, happy to know that at least one daughter would go to bed each night with more than cold gari in her belly.*

This saddened us, this sibling separation, but we couldn't take them all on, could we? We—a chemist, a botanist turned floral stylist—were hardly millionaires. We lived an average middle-class New Jersey 'burb life: a two-story colonial with a three-car drive and ballooning mortgage payments, two car notes paid off, the other, not so much. Our new aunty understood, took the balance of the thirty thousand dollars in fees we agreed upon, told us it would help them, told us this was the way it was done "back home." One child lifted up and up till they returned and lifted their whole family out of shantytown *quartiers*, out of thatch huts, out of hollowed and hungry lives.

We nodded in understanding.

Our Girl's family would be our family, we told her.

How could it be otherwise?

II

We were finally a family. Finally! Well, not quite. An adjustment period was to be expected, after all. For weeks, Our Girl roamed our home merely touching things, eyes saucered, while we followed her hopefully with our own. She was fascinated by *bling* (usage courtesy of a *How to Talk to Your Pre-Teen* pamphlet, just a coin-toss pick from the multitude of parenting ebooks, magazine articles, and podcasts we devoured). *Bling*: our Waterford crystal vases, the gold-leaf lion-head knobs of an armoire, even the gleaming touchscreen interface of our chrome Whirlpool washer. We took to wearing our shimmery baubles and finery indoors, pantomiming our movements—exaggerated yawns and back stretches that dangled Tiffany bracelets and satin-finish wristwatches, anything to draw her near. We craved her approbation. Anxiously laid shiny objects at her feet like penitents. *Did she like her new room?* (kitted out in cotton-candied furls of pink). *Were her patent leather Mary Janes too tight?* (the sizes her aunty Gladys emailed had been as off the mark as that miserable winter coat she had bought the girl).

In retrospect, it strikes us as hideous, our bottomless need for her validation, when we should have striven for her love. Back then we needed a win, we habitual gold star scholars, six-figure earners, C-suite careerists. Yet for years, among the Forjindams, the Atanganas, the Ngangmutas of our Cameroonian clique, we had been failures, reproductive underachievers. In another time, another wife might discreetly have been proffered by some well-meaning village aunty, oh so solicitous about maintaining the family line. Ours was a tribe where marriage and procreation went hand in hand, peopled by descendants of rural *gran-grans* accustomed to measuring their worth by the number of progeny, like so many sacks of cacao. Although Western diplomas brought Western mind-sets—and for couples such as we, a Western wife—remnants of old ways persist.

"Habi white women no sabi born pickin? Habi nah the man who no get bedroom power?" our so-called friends conjectured in whispers as they dandled chubby infants or noshed on palm-oily *tsetse* plantain at every born-house but our own. Among our New York social set, it was somehow worse: we were the definition of mediocre, an average Joe and Jane. There were our co-op neighbors, the Talbots—childless by choice, a couple who booked open-jaw journeys around the globe, toting that mock-croc vegan luggage from Bali to Madagascar, while we watered their fire escape philodendrons. Then the chef-owners at our favorite bistro, Tomas and Didier, devastated yet resilient after a childhood friend reneged on her promise to be their birth mother, to easy-bake-oven their offspring.

But the *poor, poor barren* Salikis were finally a family. Gone from duo to trio. And after nine bumpy, *oops*-riddled months; we were getting the hang of things with the evidence to prove it: snapshots on IG; thousands of page views for Bringing Up Baby/Bébé/Mtoto/Bimbo, our interracial, multicultural child-rearing blog. No longer would we press our faces longingly against the windows of our friends' high-gloss social media lives, their rosy cheeks smushed together for family pics on powdery slopes in Gstaad. No more *namaste* envy as coworkers regaled us with "Mommy and Me Goat Yoga" tales too precious for words. We too would be chronic chroniclers. If alien life forms explored our planet eons from now, there would be irrefutable proof, found footage of our happy family: at the pumpkin patch, schmoozing with mall Santas, attending any number of calendared events at the Children's Museum of Manhattan enrichment series. We were building our own exhibit of sorts, a collection of report cards and other artifacts, often lacquered and laminated, shining, as if under glass.

• • •

The corridors of Highland Terrace Middle School were circuitous and maple-wooded, we held hands as we Hansel and Greteled our way through this educational IKEA in search of the principal's office. We had been summoned for a parent-teacher conference to discuss our precocious child's "special needs." In truth, we were practically preening, prepared for our late-life parenting to be lauded as ultramodern, if not downright revolutionary.

"There you are, Mr. and Mrs. Saliki." A secretary sidled up on slipper-heeled feet, ushering us into the cool hush of another woodland-paneled chamber where Principal Artemis sat in state behind a coffin of a desk. Her brow was pinched behind dark cat's-eye glasses. We sat where we were instructed to.

"It's customary to begin these meetings with some pleasantries, with chitchat," she said, "yet the circumstances that led me to call you here are of such a serious nature. Well, I can see no other way but to get right to the heart of the matter."

Here, she paused. But we were trained observers, habituated to gathering facts, empirical evidence, before formulating shaky conclusions. Inwardly, steeling ourselves to fight for our child. Outwardly, we leaned forward slightly, to indicate a tepid interest and nothing more. She seemed taken aback, hesitated a moment, then said:

"Well, your daughter has excelled academically here at Highland

Terrace, in spite of some initial concerns about her ability to adjust to our expectations, the high level of rigor required of our young scholars. We've done everything in our power to welcome her, given her less-fortunate upbringing. We do make every effort to create a culture of inclusivity."

"Inclusivity?" we echoed. Yes, no doubt they thought they did. There were two Indian students from Uttar Pradesh, a half-Czech Latina, as well as ongoing relations with a sister school in Qingdao, China. And yes, there was Our Girl, in no way "less-fortunate," we had guaranteed at least that.

"Yes, inclusivity," said Artemis, forging on. "Progressive, in fact. But even we have our limits. I'm not sure what type of behavior was tolerated at your daughter's previous institutions but here at Highland there are some practices that we simply cannot tolerate. Your daughter has been, how to phrase this, *procuring* the belongings of others."

"Procuring!" one of us repeated angrily, jaw clenched tight to cage epithets in three languages and a dialect or two.

"You mean stealing?" said the other, attempting to comprehend what was all too apparent from the tight mask of disdain on the principal's face.

"Well, no. We've conducted our own internal investigations and have no evidence of that. Yet there have been complaints from a number of parents. Regarding items found missing from their homes. Items later noted in your daughter's possession."

"This is ridiculous," we cried out. "And why exactly are we here? If she's not 'stealing,' how did she—"

"She claims they were gifts. From male students who were interested in her."

"So a few moon-eyed teenage boys gave her 'gifts.' And you called us in here for that?!"

We rose in ire.

Her voice rose as well. "Mr. and Mrs. Saliki! Please understand. These items were family heirlooms: Dr. Donovan's ruby tie clip; a diamond clasp passed down in the Connelly's family for generations. Worth thousands of dollars. Priceless."

"Where are these items? Certainly not in our home."

"I don't imagine she would just leave these things hanging around in plain sight, would she? Your daughter is a very clever girl."

"Not by this account," we replied, our backs up, already striding toward the exit.

"But there's more," she says haltingly, yet her steepled hands are a cathedral of holier-than-thou condemnation. "Some of the young men. Well, they say she does things, sexual things, for these items."

"They say, they say," we parroted, cawing with bitter mirth, well versed in the cutting power of whispers made truth.

We were done then. Her imploring explanations rang on but we were out of earshot and out the door. Only after we had tossed off the requisite threats to call our attorneys, cried foul regarding Our Girl's token race status, when really all we wanted was to take her home and make sure she was safe. You see, she was damaged when we got her, Our Girl. Something Aunty Gladys had neglected to mention lest we contract some "buyer's remorse." Imagine! It had come out in family therapy. There was an uncle, we learned. She was only four years old.

We transferred her out of Highland Terrace and she has continued to excel marvelously. Of course, we talked to her that evening about the allegations. She cried. We cried. There were hugs. And for the first time in the four years she had lived with us, instead of "Mama Saliki" and "Papa Saliki," she called us Mom and Dad. Our family was made flesh. Knit together in adversity.

How could it be otherwise?

III

We did our best by Our Girl. There are those, perhaps some of the very neighbors who open-arm welcomed us with casseroles and plates heaped high with homemade brownies, who now tut-tut and give quotes to reporters skulking behind our rose bushes. But let us take you to the beginning of the end.

It all started when they took the Whirlpool. Burly men in overalls daintily rang our doorbell, asked permission to come in *please* like they were popping over for afternoon tea. Something innocuous and neighborly like Earl Grey. The ones that took the Tesla were far less courteous; they disappeared it in the nighttime while we lay fitfully in our beds dreaming of canceled credit cards and bills come due.

We were having a few financial woes.

Spare us your condemnation, your condescension. Let's have a little look-see at the red-stamped envelopes of Mastercard/Visa/American Express statements in your study drawer. No worries, we'll wait. Look, we did our best in the face of career setbacks. Who knew a senior R&D chemist for General Mills could be downsized after twenty-two loyal years? People were still eating their Wheaties. Someone was always after those Lucky Charms. And the demand for artfully arranged florals had never been particularly high in our corner of this nominally Garden State. So, things were tight, yet we were hopeful. We weren't keeping up with the jet-setter Joneses. But we were keeping our obligations. People think Bono and Bill Gates are supporting the continent; they have no idea that it's us. Families like ours sending millions in remittances so cousin Manfred can have that corrective eye operation or paying the school fees for little Arabella in the village. That was us, our burden to bear.

You have to understand how preoccupied we were back then. How desperate. Our Girl was seventeen years old, her sights set on an Ivy whose price tag we could no longer afford. So, we were slightly relieved when she said she wanted a gap year, a timeout to live life for a bit. We were proud of this young woman (when had she become such a woman, all hips and height?). She was better even than we had raised her to be, helping out around the house on weekends after we had to let the maid go. When had she learned about rinse cycles and presoaks or how to use all those special vacuum attachments? We had never even made her make her own bed.

She got a job. And two weeks later gave us an envelope thick with cash, just *a little something to help out around the house.* We didn't know where the money came from. Maybe, we didn't want to know where the money came from. She was smart, she was enterprising, she was Our Girl.

This went on for months. Till two weeks ago, Aunty Gladys was arrested. There are allegations of human trafficking and slavery and forced labor. A special prosecutor. Horrific testimonies from children she had placed with Cameroonian families all over the United States. One girl in Houston was forced to sleep on a pallet in the family's garage from the age of eight, tasked with whipping up all the meals and caring for three preschool tots and keeping the house spick-and-span. A boy in Chicago was being sexually abused by the man of the house. Allegedly, Aunty Gladys would make her rounds among illiterate and desperate villagers, have them sign ad hoc employment contracts, filling their heads with pipe dreams and promises of their child's educational advancement and monetary support for them too. The courts contend that none of the children were actually sent to school. That they were little more than indentured servants at their employers' beck and call day in and day out. The nominal pay they received (a pittance really at thirty dollars a week) was funneled back to their parents only after Aunty Gladys received her 50 percent processing fee. It was all coming to light.

Another light flashes beyond the gilded confines of our home.

We have been closeted here since the scandal broke. Blackout curtains drawn tight against the flash of camera bulbs.

The article on our family was in the *Post* today.

We are Page Six fodder, an exposé chockful of doggerel and grainy, long-lens shots.

In the paper there are pictures of "the house that whoring built," our rather unflattering driver's license photos, and screen captures from Our Girl's website, Comely Cleaners, where she offers maid services— topless, they gleefully report. A service allegedly offered to half the neighborhood, at a discounted "friends and family" rate, no less.

She had the "decency" to call on us last night. To warn us in person.

"Why would you say those things, honey?" we cried. Broken. Gawping at her from the lumpy remove of our Chesterfield sofa.

"Because I needed to," she said simply, her voice dry and crisp as fresh bills. She was standing by the credenza, shoogling a glass of blue-label whiskey that she had poured herself with an ease of manner that bespoke habit. She drank. She savored.

We sat dry-mouthed, dumb for moments, before we remembered ourselves and spoke, said, "But we love you, we've treated you like our own. Haven't we always been good to you? Given you everything you deserved?" Our arms swept through the air, wands waving over the home we had magicked together, the shimmery mirage of gold-framed family photos glimmering from atop the baby grand: Our Girl in chaps, blue-ribboned and gleaming, the glitzy lot of us—in sequined gowns, tuxedoed, at a charity gala with *His Honor*, the mayor.

Our Girl looked about her, taking in all of it, scanning past her own packed bags by the door before her gaze landed on us once more. Her eyes narrowed. Ours opened. We looked at a woman who seemed to see right through us.

"Yes. You took me from my loving family so you could make my life better, right?" she said. "You bought the best and taught me to want the best. To need and breathe it like air. You should be thrilled: the money they gave me for the story will pay for college and then some. Maybe I can parlay this into a book. Maybe a movie. Wish me well."

She departed then and we clung to each other. Shivering and pondering in the waning hours of the evening. Had we made mistakes? Perhaps. Maybe we'd spoiled her with feasts, unaware there'd be famine. There were lofty expectations for her. But nothing untoward. Our parental sins replicated in cul-de-sacs cross the country. But what had we done to deserve this? Deep in thought, we withdrew to our master suite, waiting there for us a cream linen envelope on the nightstand. Tucked therein: a diamond clasp with an eagle insignia, a ruby-studded tie clip, and a note in Our Girl's meticulous handwriting that read simply:

> *To Mom and Dad,*
> *For your troubles.*
> *Your perfect daughter,*
> *Winsome*

Volume II: Their Girl

I

I give good read. *Mais je suis rien commes des autres.* Nothing like them. Those *poor, poor* telethon kids you scribble letters to and force-feed *poto-poto* rice "for just ten cents a day." Fly-haloed. Swollen tum-tums begging for your pretax dollars. You give and you give and you give again. #SaveOurKids. #BecauseYouCare. No, I am nothing like them, but I made your heartstrings twang with tabloid tales of my liberation from the Salikis, who took me when I was just a small *titi* and made me Their Girl.

I was thirteen years old when she came for me, Mrs. Fontep *aka* Ngando *aka* Ndukong. First choice had been my follow-back, Arabella. Last cocoa in our family—age eight but could pass for the type of cuddly five-year-old you and your *madame* know from commercials where Happy Children™ eat Cheerios™ and Lucky Charms™ and all the world is *shine-shine*. Bella was *très mignon*—a doll-baby with long, silky Hausa hair and a sweet as *bonbon* manner so unlike me, my *maman*'s "*wahala pickin*."

"Perfect, perfect," said Mrs. Ndukong, eyes squinted and calculating.

At the center of our parqueted front parlor, Bella was twirling slowly for inspection in a dress *Maman* had fashioned from the remnants of an old *okrika* dress, its tattered lace made fine again by her hand. *Maman* just sat there next to Mrs. Ndukong, quiet as a *muet-muet*, head hanging low as overripe paw-paw. I was setting the table for our guest's meal. My ever-watchful *grande sœur*, Frieda, monitored from the kitchen doorway—neither in nor out.

"Does she speak proper English?" asked Mrs. Ndukong, suddenly sniffing her nose as if illiteracy had a pit toilet stench and we reeked.

Do we speak proper English? Swine-beef! I wanted to tell that fatty *bobolo*, "*Nous sommes bilingues.*" My family had lived in Douala for ten years now since *Maman* had come to make market—so we spoke "proper" English *and* "proper" French *and* pidgin *and* Franglais. Not like Mrs. Ndukong, with her *pili-pili* bush pronunciation grinding up "proper" into "pro-paah."

I looked to Frieda, who looked at me, and shook her head no. So I folded my arms and sucked my teeth.

Mrs. Ndukong gave me some kind of eye.

"Do you have something to say, Zo . . . what is this one's name again?" she turned and asked *Maman*, who, without lifting her gaze from the ground, said, "Don't mind her, *Madame*. That one is always talking."

"I only wanted to say that food is ready, *Tantine*." I capped the lie with my best imitation Bella curtsy.

"No, no," Mrs. Ndukong replied. "I get plenty appointments *dem*. I no get time for *chop*."

At this, *Maman* finally lifted her head. We all stared. For weeks she had been preparing. *Chey! Frieda have you dry-cleaned this floor? See me this girl. You want Madame to think we have no manners? Wahala pickin carry that new serving dish and go tchuk am high for shelf where Arabella no fih reach.* She had been bartering her skills for weeks to make this dinner perfect. To buy *gari* that was a fine gold dust. Miraculously weevil-free *sef-sef*! For goat meat to put in the *egusi* stew, the butcher's wife received three Vlisco Dutch wax attires sewn *gratuit*. *Hmph*. What made her too good for the bongo fish we usually ate it with? And why did we have to make *show-show* for people who were begging *us* for a child? People who were thiefing my sister.

"You'll not sit and eat, *small-small*?" *Maman* asked. "I made the food special, secret family ingredients."

"No, no. I cannot," Mrs. Ndukong repeated.

Maman frowned.

We smiled.

Savoring the thought.

Licking our lips.

Our bellies biting.

"Very well, Madelaine," Mrs. Ndukong finally said, sighing. "I can see you went to some trouble. Pack the food. I will taste it and dash the rest to my night-watch."

She smiled at her generosity.

I was vexed *sootay*. This woman with all her *juro-juro* chins wobbling. Had she ever missed a meal in her whole life? Making me a *langa* dog sniffing for scraps in my own home!

I took the plate to the kitchen as instructed, but scraped half into a bowl for my sisters and me to eat behind the house. The rest I put in *Maman's* best new dish. Mixed in some tap water to puff it up again. Placed it on the floor between my legs, squatting to add in some of my own secret family ingredient. *Hehehe.*

I was humming when I returned to the parlor to find Mrs. Ndukong up on her feet, pacing and shouting. I thought of her "special" soup and squared my shoulders, ready to deny or to fight. But I saw Arabella hiding behind *Maman's* skirt, crying until catarrh was bubbling from her nose.

"You tried to give me an *eboah*!" said Mrs. Ndukong, stomping toward *Maman*, prompting Frieda to come stand by her side with the stick we used for killing rats clutched in one hand. Mrs. Ndukong glared at my mother, then my sister, said, *"Che, che, che!* See me these tricksters! A whole *eboah*. How manage?"

I forgot to mention that perfect Bella had a slight defect—a tiny limp, no worse than any other kids we knew in the *quartier*—with their *bend-bend* legs and rocking-pony gaits—all thanks to poorly dosed polio vaccinations at the free government clinic. Mrs. Ndukong yelled some more but *Maman*, who knew how to make market if she knew anything at all, began her best *buyam-sellam* spiel. She pulled me forward. Sold Mrs. Ndukong on how strong and hardworking I was.

"Madelaine, I don't need a housegirl—"

"She's top of her class—"

I had been. Before I was kicked out of school for lack of school fees.

"She looks a bit old—"

"She's only ten, *Madame*."

Mrs. Ndukong lifted an eyebrow.

"Sorry, I meant eleven, her birthday just passed."

"Hmph. She will do."

A month later I was shivering by a fireplace that looked like it could roast me whole like a goat. I was tired. I was hungry. And a little angry. I was what the Salikis wanted. And maybe a bit more than they bargained for.

Wasn't I worth it?

II

"How now, *petite sœur*? How you d—"

My sister Frieda's face was stuck midquestion—all googly-eyed, hanging *mop* showing her gap teeth. Our shaky WhatsApp vid connection kept sputtering like a beat-up *clando* taxi at the motor park. We had been talking for an hour and usually got cut off by now because Frieda always forgot to top up her phone minutes. In the hush, I heard the Mother coming. Or rather the swish of the high blond ponytail that forever swung behind her, agitating the air. She was in the open door to my bedroom, the one I wasn't allowed to lock until I officially turned sixteen. Two years from now by the Salikis' count. Two years ago by mine.

"Oh, no. The screen froze again?" she said. "Do they need another cell phone, sweetie? I told your dad we should've shelled out for the upgrade. He can be such a cheapskate sometimes. I think it's from growing up with little to nothing."

"It's fine, *Madame*," said Frieda, sharing a look with me since the man in question was the son of an exiled minister, alleged embezzler of millions of francs from the government till. The whereabouts of that loot are still a mystery, but the Salikis had enough to be generous; just last week they air-mailed my family laptops and an iPhone with all types of social media apps preloaded so we could keep in touch.

"Please, call me Jessica," the Mother said.

"Thank you, *Madame* Jessica," my sister replied. Frieda would never call her by her given name. Back home, we respected our elders. No matter how silly they were. Besides, Frieda didn't believe half the things I told her about the Mother because real parents never teetered on your BLΛƆKPIИK bedspread to practice putting on lip gloss with you, or asked you about your period and your feelings, or sashayed around in your Acne jeans humming because they've still "got it." Never. Ever.

Just the day before, she was blasting Kamer hip-hop, telling me, "This new Jovi track *na die!*"

Seriously?

Frieda doesn't understand. The Salikis had plenty. In the beginning, they would always be hovering around me. Showing off their *fine-fine* clothing and their *fine-fine* jewelry like I had never seen such things in my life. Like I was from the bush! The Mother always swishing her hair in my face like I couldn't buy my own horse tail at the mall! But Frieda would stare at screen caps of my perfect pink bedroom and curse me *fine-fine* for complaining. Tell me if I had stayed in Cameroon, I would have ended up like *Maman* with three kids, three different fathers, none of them her husband.

Frieda doesn't have a clue. It's a grind. *Na hard work* being one of the Happy Children™. Constant extracurrics: ballet on Tuesdays, riding lessons on Thursdays, daily violin, and an English tutor to help me speak better "American." Then there's the school *palava*— from Highland Terrace to Carmichael Prep—always *palava*. The run-hide-fight active-shooter drills in halls full of strapping blond boys who'd sooner bang-bang shoot you down than date you. Their love on reserve for roving packs of perky girls: Amber (all twelve of her), Tiffani/y (the two with a *y* and six with *i* that she is), all looking right through you till you got the perfect Gucci knockoff and hair extensions like Kims K through Z. Everything air-kiss fake and phony. But at least, some things come naturally. I was great at maths, excuse me, mathematics, or more accurately AP algebra came easy. Like my *maman*, I had a head for figures.

Soon as they knew, the Salikis signed me up for Future Entrepreneurs Club. And Mathletics for good measure.

• • •

My sister and *Madame* Jessica chatted for a few more minutes. Mainly, Frieda's "thank you, thank yous" for the new clothes sent to her and the rest of my "six" siblings. Mrs. Ndukong was masterful at supplying official-looking documents from various boarding schools, at extracting ever-mounting school fees. Unlike me, Frieda had problems lying about make-believe kin. She made show-and-tell for the Mother, gathering Arabella and some small yam-heads from the *quartier* together for Skype sessions. Called me a *lie-lie pickin*. Though it didn't keep her from selling all that extra clothing to help fill *Maman*'s new stall in the market—a side business selling American goods. *Maman* got a mean markup. We got something just for us. But sometimes Frieda's boyfriend Boniface helped manage the store when *Maman* was busy sewing. I didn't trust him with a register full of our hard-earned *nkap*. And I didn't bite my tongue about saying so. *Ey-ey!* The yam-head was a cutpurse—okay, okay—that's "pickpocket" in American. *Former cutpurse*, Frieda said. Then she said I was a hypocrite. My hands were way down deep in the Salikis' pockets, *no be so?*

"Hypocritical? *Mais non, grande sœur*," I said. "*Entrepreneurial*. That's me."

Wasn't I worth it?

III

I did what I had to. For myself. For my real family's future. Mrs. Ndukong discovered *Maman*'s kiosk and demanded her cut. Grubby hands in every sauce pot. And the well was running dry. The Salikis were struggling. So I got *entrepreneurial*.

It began with heartbreak. One of those strapping blond boys finally took a liking. *Imagine! An American boyfriend of my very own!* But for months his gaze kited over me in school corridors. I went dateless at three dances. After a time, it dawned on me. I was too dark for daylight hours. I was low, felt invisible. But I yam what I yam so I rallied. And soon another came along—big, brawny—people hailing from somewhere in the country's big-belted waistband. I looked at him and saw plenty: fattened calves, amber waves of grain. He looked at me and saw exotica: spears, teats—everything jutting. He would screw me for novelty, his wifey-to-be a corn-fed sweetie. But this time round I would get something. Treasured. A keepsake. My own little piece of America.

These trinkets lured cornpone princesses in pink-sequined UGGs. Girls gone gaga for *show-show* and bling. Amber H's family rec room was unexpectedly the perfect recruiting ground for my start-up. Too grown for pillow fights and pinky swears, she was hosting an "ironic" slumber party. There we were, lounging in the most cerebral man cave I'd ever seen, walls lined with walnut shelves faced in glass, recessed lights showcasing her dad's collection of intricately carved Meerschaum pipes and Japanese netsuke—miniature demons, Buddhas, dragons sculpted from ivory, from boxwood. Not a pool table or arcade game in sight. Yawn.

Even the eats were ridiculously posh; we noshed on all things artisanal. No mixes—Chex, trail, or otherwise—for this sleepover spread. Amber H's parents were known foodies, weekday meals featuring yummy wordplay like Taco Tuesdays and Stir Fry Days.

At Amber H's imperious behest, we arranged ourselves in a circle on the floor, cross-legged, seated "Indian style" according to Bavishni, who'd insisted, "It's not racist when *I* say it. And no way are we calling it lotus pose like we're Lululemon yogis. Appropriate much?"

Amber H, who considered herself "super-woke" for inviting half our school's POC population to her silk-pajama-clad shindig and for that one time she retweeted #blacklivesmatter "protesting" yet another dystopian shooting by public servants sworn to protect and serve, said, "You're not that kind of 'Indian,' Vish."

"I think it's pronounced 'Native American,'" I chimed in, between yeasty mouthfuls of ragged bread torn from a pumpernickel bowl brimming with spinach dip. This drew a chuckle from her bestie Amber C and a scowl from Amber H, an omen that someone would pay for that infraction later.

Amber H broke out a Carmichael yearbook for a death match round of Marry-Kiss-Kill that left an OCD Amber C sniffling in the laundry room as she stress-sorted whites and coloreds. The "Aryan Wash Cycle" is what I called it once the maid was let go and that particular chore fell to me. Next came a round of Never-Have-I-Ever and I could see the secret side looks hinting at devious pregame plans but no one was brazen enough to game the game and suss out if the rumors from my old school were true. Never have I ever "stolen from my boyfriend's home."

Try to put me in your trick bag? Never have I ever fallen for it. But midround, my phone beeped with a check-in text from Jessica and it was downright Pavlovian how girls hungrily eyed my bedazzled next-gen cellie.

"Where'd you get that?" the hive voice asked, the gaggle of girls sharpening their nails.

I shrugged a coy "this ole thing," even as I toyed on and on with apps, letting it shine bright in the low light. "It's from a wish list online. I've got a whole bunch of them for high-end boutiques like Farfetch, Matches, Shopbop—you name it."

"Wish lists? But who buys you the stuff? And what do they get for it?" A volley of voices pinged questions all at once; some of these girls still sucked their thumbs when they slept, some had graduated to sucking other things. I could see all the seedy, no-tell motel thoughts running through their heads. Hilarious.

"All I do is chat with them. Online. On the phone. That's it. It's called *findom*, for secure men who just love showering us ladies with gifts." I scanned the room, giving a knowing smile to those who leaned in, eager to learn the how-tos of securing that bag, then said, "I tell guys my weekly minimums from the get-go, so they really know I'm worth it. So they really feel the pinch."

Don't @ me with your outrage. *Je suis rien commes des autres.* I'm a hustler. You were warned from the start. I'm no victim, I made men pay for the mere suggestion of what my uncle tried to take for free. Back home, these tit-for-tat, transactional relationships between men and women were *de rigueur.* Future Entrepreneurs Club hipped me to the blunt economics of it all. Women cashed in on the wasting asset of their youth, all too aware of its inevitable depreciation in the years to come. They instinctively understood the "time value of money" principle, how money makes money in the here and now. Why wait on a degree in an already uncertain economy, when guaranteed capital was only a flirty smile with Daddy Warbucks away? Call it an investment in your future self. They offered companionship to wealthy older boyfriends otherwise known as "sponsors," "patrons," and "blessers" (these men answered prayers for new shoes, yes, but also financial solvency for tuition bills, your mother's medical bills, life). In findom we call these men paypigs or cash$laves. In findom, I told Amber H and Co., we refined this business model, no sweaty-sheet commerce required.

Many of the girls were hooked. They wanted so much more than Daddy's Little Girl deserves. So, I taught them how to find spanking-new daddies. Took a cut—a modest 20 percent finder's fee—for the connections I facilitated. It worked so well I set up a dark web site. And soon another for sexy maid services, where a girl could cash in on a giggly *Oopsy-daisy, I dropped the feather duster,* bending low to flash fishnets, saying, *Silly me. How clumsy.* It was just that easy. This is a land where homemade XXX equals endorsements, a hip-hop hubby, and an iPhone app of your very own. Sex always, always sells.

Question was: how to keep Mrs. Fontep *aka* Ngando *aka* Ndukong out of my profit margins? She was a truffle pig for money stashes, rooting out hidden revenue streams. Frieda told me she ambushed *Maman* at her shop, confiscating top-notch merchandise I'd shipped the month before. She was relentless. She had to be stopped. So, I gathered intel, touched base with some of the other children she had airdropped in barely vetted homes across the US.

A girl in Houston. *Sleeping on a lumpy pallet? That cannot lie!*
A boy in Chicago. *They touched you down there? You don't say?*
Horrific tales, all.

My mission? Accomplished. Had all the ammunition needed and then some.

Don't judge. It was war. Kill or be killed.

So by the time they took the Whirlpool, I was ready. A sugar daddy client knew a guy who knew a guy who worked at the *Post*. A week later, Aunty Gladys was arrested. There were allegations of human trafficking and slavery and forced labor. A special prosecutor appointed.

My interview is in the *Post* today. My side hustles too salacious to pass up in print. It was publicity for my businesses—Comely Cleaners set to double its customer base.

It really was never meant to be about the Salikis. My story is my own to tell.

Said as much when I talked to them last night.

Listening as they blubbered on and on about all the things they'd done for me.

For me? Seriously? It was me who made them a family. I'm the one who made them real. "Wasn't I worth it?" I asked. "I was snatched up from my loving family so yours could be complete. All this talk of giving me the American dream. Then just like that, you're raiding my college fund."

"We had a mortgage to pay!" they cried. "You needed a roof over your head!"

"I needed a future," I said finally. "And now I've made sure I'll have one."

I left them to their tears and seltzer water.

Tucked away in my hotel bed, I dreamed of better. Maybe I could parlay my story into a book. Or a Lifetime movie at the very least. I pictured the opening credits.

Based upon a true story. With my true name in bright, blazing lights . . .

                                        ZORA.

Rain Check at MomoCon

There is a crush of Stormtroopers, Men of Steel, and Optimus Primes milling around the cavernous confines of the Javits Center. Surrounded by freaks and geeks, Astrid Atangana wonders how she and her friends—the self-styled *Nyanga Girlz*—come across to the Comic-Con crowd. Mbola, rocking grills and street gear, calling herself "Fly Girl: Superman's dope-ass cousin from the hood." Mimi, in the Psylocke cosplay costume, preordered from China a full month in advance. And her, a too-tall Black girl in a too-short red kimono. Wearing bifocals, no less. She takes off her glasses. She cringes, thinking about the Princeton admissions letter, secreted away in a notebook, in the far reaches of her knapsack, then secures the bag's straps, along with the side-slung holster of her *katana*, for what feels like the kajillionth time.

"Batman has a bomb booty," Mimi opines, twirling an eely purple hair strand that slithers and coils around her index finger. Her flinty eyes are fixated. *Medusan*, Astrid thinks, filled with equal parts fascination and disgust, watching her friend watching yet another guy.

"Which Batman?" Mbola asks. "There are like a billion Dark Knight wannabes up in this piece. Look at these clone wars muthas. Him, him, him." She points an accusatory diamante-crusted stiletto nail, its gold gun charm swinging wildly, at each and every offender within eyeshot. "Folks is so basic."

"That don't matter if they hot," Mimi says, jerking her head to their left. "Dude, right there, could totally get it," answering their blank looks with a rapid-fire whisper, "him, the retro, Adam West-y one, over there by the Halo booth," then loudly exclaims, "Oh my God, Astrid! Don't look straight at him."

Astrid is already looking straight at him. Staring, in fact. Mbola rolls her eyes in exasperation, yet all too soon she is staring too. Batman catches their gaze and gives them all an even-toothed, Tic Tac grin. Mimi denies him a smile. Instead she turns away, flips her synthetic tresses, then tosses him a knowing, coquettish look over her shoulder. *Classic Mimi.* Astrid hopes he's worth it; hopes she gets a bang for her buck. The girl spent two weeks' worth of pay to buy her wig—its shock of violet locks had to be *the exact shade of purple* as her costume; the cheapo wigs at the beauty supply in the West Orange mall where they all worked deemed insufficiently "Con-worthy."

A schlubby East Asian Boy Wonder sidles over and palms Batman's left butt cheek, his wandering hand partially obscured by a waterfall of midnight blue polyester. *Manhandling*, Astrid thinks, her brain continuing a weeklong streak of randomly churning out *M* words, morphing her into some Tourette tic-ish freak. It was weird but strangely familiar, like the month after their class trip to see *Hamilton* on Broadway when quotidian conversations tempted her to segue into song. That month, talk of Batman's heinie might have triggered wordless humming of Sir Mix-a-Lot's '90s throwback hit "Baby Got Back" under her breath. Or at least some bars from the Nicki remix.

Mimi is glaring at the Dynamic Duo now. "Look, Astrid. It's one of your fairy tale *up-the-rear* endings."

Mbola sniggers her approval of the diss.

Maleficents, Astrid thinks. She mentally kicks herself, again, for ever, *EVER* sharing her slash fan-fiction with these so-called friends. For months, they had cracked on her about Luke Skywalker letting Han Solo stroke his *light saber* during long and lonely desert nights on "Brokeback Tatooine." She had almost given up on writing before she met Young Yoon at Arcania, their mall's comic book store.

He was the one—the only one—who hadn't laughed. Instead, he had pulled out a sketch pad and shown her his storyboards, shared panel upon panel of darkly rendered swordplay. The only text was his name in Hangul: 영윤. *They're pretty much just mimes right now. I need someone to give them a voice. Can you help with that, Astrid?* And Astrid, knowing what it was like to be kept mute, had said yes. He was upstairs right now, manning their spot in artists' alley. The one they had spent months scraping together funds for in hopes that they could really make a go of all this.

Silently, Astrid packs up her ever-growing collection of Jetstream uni-ball pens, her glasses, and finally her notebook, its pages full of secret letters, story scribblings, and haiku descriptions of passersby: *Rotund Robin comes / Caped Crusader smiles, grateful / Their night play begins.*

"Where you goin'?" Mimi demands, in a voice that spoke of razor blades stashed under the tongue. Mimi was tiny, but in an instant her body could radiate this rude-gal aggro energy that Astrid had all too often taken the brunt of. Astrid's tongue would grow heavy with blood and conciliatory words yet unsaid, only for Mimi to flip the script entirely and threaten to "cut a bitch" just for looking at Astrid "funny," stank-eye connoisseur that she was, nobody was allowed to step to her crew, and "crew" meant Astrid too. It boggled the mind.

"Just heading to the booth right quick," says Astrid. *Booth* is a misnomer really, it was just a table they were sharing with another vendor, some dude hawking a cheesy bootleg comic about homicidal bees called *Stinger*.

"Yeah, you tell the *booth* I said hi," Mbola says, then turns to Mimi, "'cause that *booth* is fine as shit." Mbola has a crush on Young Yoon. An insistent one. She thinks he looks like Night—the humanoid robot cum heartthrob from her all-time-fave Japanese soap opera, *Zettai Kareshi*. She also thinks Astrid is secretly dating him. She is a dim bulb: her belief in Astrid's frequent assertions that they are "just friends" flickers off, and on, and off again, fickly.

"You hear me, Astrid?" asks Mbola. "I said tell Young Money I said 'make that paper.' Get that shmoney. Get it. Get it." She's dancing and dipping low as she chants the last of it, doing a little butt bounce that would have been innocuous on anyone else but in those tight, low-rider jeans with her disproportionate "all my height went to my donk" derriere. Wow. Just wow.

"Shut up, Mbola," Mimi commands. "Come on, Astrid. Don't be mad, girl. You promised. The panel, remember? The open buffet of K-town hotties. I'll buy you some boba after. You know I know what you like."

The panel that afternoon featured stars from *Boys Over Flowers*, Mimi's all-time-fave Korean soap. Astrid had signed up to be Mimi's Rosetta Stone wing-woman, helping pull guys with the few Korean phrases Young had taught her. Simple stuff, really, like "hello," *annyeong*, and "goodbye," *annyeong*.

"*Annyeong*," Astrid says, fidgeting with her *katana* strap, watching the growing frown on Mimi's face. "I'll be back. Just checking in to see if we sold anything."

She doesn't want to come back, doesn't want to return to the cutting laughter and faux camaraderie of these frenemies, but she knows she will. She is Elastigirl (cue sad trombones), bending and contorting to the will of others in a single fold. She hates this about herself, knowing that she will give up all this comic book *mishegoss* and cave under seismic maternal pressures to head off to an Ivy far, far away, leaving Young in the more experienced hands of Mbola. It doesn't take X-ray vision to see this. But for now, in this fantasy land, nothing is decided. She is surrounded by mild-mannered accountants, data entry specialists, computer analysts—assorted neckbeards. All shedding their daytime skins, thrilling to their secret identities in a dreamscape free from the mundanities of rumored downsizings, late mortgage payments, and vacant relationships. For a brief time, they all are heroes. Her too.

• • •

That morning, Astrid marveled at the surprising ease of her escape from home. As strongholds go, the Atangana household is rather well fortified, its days regimented by a rigorously upheld agenda of activities sanctioned by her mother. The totemic family calendar marks them all: "Saturday, October 27, 10am–2pm: Mrs. Atangana—church dinner planning meeting // Mr. Atangana—golf with colleagues at Fairlawn // Astrid—college prep with M.F." M.F. is Mimi, with whom she is supposedly prepping for next week's college campus tour. As alibis go, Mimi is pretty ideal. She is a play-cousin, from a suitable Cameroonian family that attends the same church as her own and who, above all, possesses the same immigrant values: education and hard work. The Forjindams own a similar beige-painted-by-numbers, prefab mansion a few blocks away from the Atanganas. Both families stoically take their steep suburban tax lumps so that their kids can grow up in nice homes, with really nice neighbors and even nicer school districts.

Mimi never makes straight As like Astrid in said schools, but she does sing soprano in their church's youth choir, the ultimate imprimatur of a "good girl." With a thrill, Astrid sometimes imagines the look on her mother's face if she ever found out that Mimi had her purity ring resized so she could slip it off effortlessly when she went out on dates. She knows what face her mother makes around Mbola already: the upturned nose, the repeated sniffing. Mbola is a distant relative of the Forjindams. She lives in East Orange, the bizarro West Orange, where her asylum-seeker parents braid hair, tend other people's lawns, and receive ill-considered hand-me-downs and hand-outs from their West Orange kin. Even further removed from making straight As than Mimi, Mbola teases Astrid for "talking white" and attends a crowded high school with metal detectors and girls named after luxury cars and liqueurs like Alizé and Lexus. Astrid's mother thinks Mbola is an unsavory influence. "Unsavory" like corrupt food left too long on a countertop.

". . . and make sure you remind Mrs. Forjindam to bring her okra stew to the church dinner this Sunday, Astrid. That *lay-lay* woman likes to 'forget' her duties on purpose," said her mother that morning, cleaving through the family room and its stuffy coterie of plastic-covered couches on her way to the garage. Astrid, her proximity alert blinking rapidly, had hurried in from the kitchen, only three steps behind the hull of her mother's retreating form.

"Astrid! *See me trouble, oh.* Where is that girl?" Her mother had stopped, midstride, suddenly sensing that perhaps she hadn't been automatically attended to.

"I'm here, Mummy," Astrid said, bending slightly at the waist, performing the obligatory obeisance that helped her push past these moments faster.

"Yes, you are. Don't forget what I told you about the dinner," said her mother, charging forward once more into the garage. Hiking up into her towering Benz S-Class, her mother ticked through her checklist: *Put dishes in washer, Astrid* (garage remote in hand, garage door lifting with the slow mechanized creak of an outdated android), *Call your grandmother, Astrid* (keys turn in the ignition, the craft readies for departure).

"Yes, Mummy," said Astrid, then again, "yes, Mummy." The last said to empty air. Her mother had finally taken off.

• • •

On the PATH train platform into the city, Young, Mimi, and Mbola had assessed Astrid's costume.

"Who you?" Mbola had asked, her tone filled with no small amount of suspicion. "What are you supposed to be?"

"What she is, is highly *kkuljaem*," Young answered, giving her his highest compliment in a worldview filled with two types of people: those noteworthy enough to be *kkuljaem*, and all the rest who were just plain *nojaem*. Astrid giggled the first time she heard the word. It sounded like "cool jam"—a chart-topping Spotify bop or the kind of artisanal preserves hipsters sourced from farmer's markets and food co-ops. Young spelled both in Korean for her: 꿀잼 (*kkuljaem*) and 노잼 (*nojaem*). More vocab for the Rosetta word bank.

Mimi gave Astrid a once-over. "She's that ninja superhero chick from their comic book."

"She's a samurai. And it's a graphic novel," said Young.

"Whatevs, superheroes don't wear glasses," said Mimi, with finality.

"What about Clark Kent or Beast?" Mbola said, eager to support her (fingers-crossed) future baby daddy, her eyes on Young, saying, "And Cyclops wears that visor thingy so he don't burn folk up with his eyes. Ooh, ooh, and what 'bout your girl Wonder Woman, Mimi, what about her?"

"Alter egos don't count," Mimi said. "When she's Wonder Woman, she's a princess and she's perfect."

As the two girls bickered, Young and Astrid swapped home evasion stories involving synchronized watches and draconian parental curfews. At the mention of his father, Young sighed repeatedly, running charcoal-stained fingers through his crazed anime hair, its spiky tufts defiant, jabbing the air excitedly like inky exclamation points. His dad, senior pastor at the biggest Korean Presbyterian church in Central Jersey, bowed a head full of gelled, upstanding Kim Jong-il hair in prayer every Sunday morning at 8 a.m., 10 a.m., and 12 o'clock services. The right Reverend Yoon had serious hair and serious plans for his son to be leader of his flock someday. Plans that did not involve Young's siblings: his sister Gi, a K-Poppy-slash-keyboard activist who flooded racist Twitter feeds with ARMY fancams and wore colorful T-shirts with sayings like "Unicorns Are My Spirit Animal," or Park, his blind older brother, who was a stellar sculler in the "engine room" of a championship eight-man rowing team. The Rev would be damned if he let his younger son, and heir apparent, succumb to a life of frivolous etching.

"You're going to have to tell your dad about the letter sooner or later," Astrid said. "You have to speak up for yourself someday, *senpai*."

"Right back at you, *kōhai*."

There were two letters actually: Young's acceptance to a fine arts program at Pratt and Astrid's to Princeton. Hers was in the notebook she carried everywhere, kept close to her chest like a breath or a promise. Young's was tucked away, alongside his art supplies, in a hidey-hole at school. Both were safeguarded from mothers who "accidentally" read your diary or fathers who sprinkled your "heathenish" artwork with holy water.

Young had sighed once again. "Look, tell her you don't want to go to Princeton. It's a great school, just not for you. Show her that life goal list of yours. What's your mother gonna do? Whip out *The Photo* again?"

The Photo was legendary among her friends, holding sway in their collective imaginations like lore of the One Ring or the Sorcerer's Stone. Astrid had first seen *The Photo* when she was ten years old, slipping peas to their dog, Cujo, under the dining room table. Her mother put her fork down and left the room. She returned with a photo—it wasn't *The Photo* yet—but her mother held it up to her face with all the import that it would soon come to hold. Astrid had grown up listening to her classmates' stories of how tricky parents guilted them into eating liver, brussels sprouts, and the like with tales of all the little children starving in Africa. Except for Astrid, there was no mystery malnourished African child behind door number two.

That child was real.

That child was a relative.

"*This is your cousin Adama*," her mother had said, pushing the photo even closer to her face. "*Look at her! Do you think she can refuse food? Do you?*" And Astrid had studied the little girl standing barefoot in a blush of red dust, yet improbably clean; clad only in a trophy-shiny Super Bowl T-shirt, donation-bin wear from a team that had forfeited their championship dreams. Adama stood there smiling, a mud brick hut behind her, an uncertain future ahead of her, and the photo became *The Photo*: her mother's insurance for her good grades—*Adama's parents could barely afford her school fees*—and good behavior—*if Adama misbehaved, she was disciplined with a caning.*

It had worked for a longer time than Astrid was willing to own up to, even to herself.

"Have you met my mother?" Astrid jokingly asked. "Answer? No, you haven't, because you know if Mrs. 'No daughter of mine is dating before marriage' catches me with a boy, I'm donezo. She's a paragon of open-mindedness. Yeah right. I'm keeping all this on the low. She'll kill me."

"Sure she will." Young's expression was still doubtful. One of his bonsai brows, so dubbed due to their bushy expressiveness, raised high.

"No, I mean it." Suddenly, Astrid had a vision, so vivid—*Mittyesque*, her mind supplies. God, she wished her life was that Technicolor, or her un-life, as it were. There she lay, her lifeless body prone with arms akimbo in a ghoulish foxtrot, in a photo labeled "Exhibit A." There was Gwendolyn, her somber older sis, the attorney—African parent–approved career #1—defending her mother in court as her brother Gerald, the doctor—African parent–approved career #2—testified about "mental duress" and "temporary insanity."

"If only she had gone to Princeton and become an engineer!" Her mother wailed as a jury of sympathetic peers nodded in understanding. Lawyer, doctor, engineer—the high holy trinity of professions blessed by African parents. *Writing graphic novels? No. Friggin'. Way.*

• • •

Astrid and Young "Money" Yoon's table is at the tail end of a strivers' row of indie comic labels, one-off prints, and handmade fabulist's figurines. For a moment, Astrid is hopeful when she sees Young talking to a guy who is leafing through their *dwindling maybe?* stack of merchandise. They were set to meet Baek Hyeon, owner of Arcania and a chain of sister stores in cities up and down the Eastern Seaboard. Baek Hyeon was big on promoting minority artists, especially fellow fans of deep-cut *doujins* and one-of-a-kind *manhwa* from the homeland like Young. Astrid had also wowed him with her Blerdy trivia. Did you know MLK was a Trekkie? Did you know Storm, weather witch extraordinaire, beat Themyscira's Finest, in a legendary cross-over smackdown? Did you know that Lois Lane was Black for a day? This homegirl hopeful jumped into a Transformoflux and got a melanin injection just to test if Superman would still marry her ebony 2.0. The more you know (cue rainbow xylo)! This was the kind of rando, *weeaboo* knowledge that triggered side-eyes from Mimi and had Mbola declaring "you ain't never gonna get a man," but Baek Hyeon got it. And "it" was going to get them a distribution deal, she hopes.

Astrid puts her glasses back on and realizes it's not Baek Hyeon, it's just Abel—the skeevy owner of another, rival comic book store.

"How big was your print run?" Astrid hears Abel ask, as she steps up to the pair, lychee bubble tea in hand.

"'Bout a thousand," Young says with puffed-chest bravado.

Astrid nearly spit-takes her boba at Young's inventive salesman-ship. They had really only printed three hundred copies of *The Seer: The Tales of Augur Brown*, a blind swordswoman—Zatoichi meets Cleopatra Jones. Augur had an eerie ability to see inside evildoers' souls and dispensed a blade-based justice according to a personal ethos loosely derived from *bushido* code and the laws of the street.

"Wow, you mean business, dude. I thought this was some sorta vanity project."

"*We* told you *we* were serious about this," Young says. "Astrid and I are a team. Her writing's gotten so good, it's like she knows my characters better than I do." Young taps a pencil against his palm for emphasis. "Her scripts keep my visuals in mind. She's an awesome collaborator."

Astrid smirks at this over-the-top praise-a-thon, she can't help herself. Later she'll have to faux-swoon into his arms, bat her eye-lashes, and sigh, "My hero. Thanks ever so kindly for saving lil' ole me from that big, bad Abel." They'd talked about this. Astrid and Young had had many a heated discussion about damsel-in-distress tropes and all the regressive gender politics lingering in geek culture. He knew better. He caught her look and the cocky curl of his upper lip said: "Bring it."

"Tell you what. I'll display a coupla copies on my shelves and go in fifty-fifty on the sales price. Deal?" says Abel, head bobbing in enthusiasm—a graying ponytail practically wagging with excitement at the thought of profits.

"I've got to discuss it with my business partner." Young looks at her, still half smirking.

"Sure, sure. You do that," Abel says, then turning to Astrid, declares, "Nice getup."

Astrid looks at his retreating Hawaiian-shirted bulk, then at Young. She raises an eyebrow.

"I know, I know. He's a chauvinist ass who only likes his girls chesty and splayed across comic book covers. Blah, blah, you said it already. Now get over it." He smiles.

They both knew about Abel's collection of *hentai* back in his storeroom—everything from *futa* to furry. His top-shelf titles held for special clientele with a taste for saucer-eyed *dakimakura* girls, kitted out in abbreviated plaid minis and Hello Kitty backpacks, opulent *oppai* bouncing as they're ravaged by slimy tentacles, in every orifice.

"Whatevs," says Astrid. Turning to go, she smiles sweetly. "BTDubz, your girl Mbola says hi."

"She's so not *kkuljaem*," Young replies.

The first time Young had called Astrid *kkuljaem*, she had giggled, then gone quiet. She'd just shown him the first draft of her script for Augur Brown's next installment. They were sitting together on a tweedy brown sofa tucked in a corner of the library, their legs inches apart but no actual contact ever made. Astrid found herself wiping suddenly clammy hands and then her glasses on the hem of her flowery summer dress. Daffodil petals swept clean one lens, then the other. Young was silent, poring through her work. When he looked up, his eyes seemed to pinball all over her. *What was he thinking? What was she thinking?* She wrote stories in the margins of textbooks: tales of a father killing his infant son to end a family curse unfolded alongside tangents and quadrants in *Bittinger's Algebra and Trigonometry: Seventh Edition with enhanced study guide*; a tale of two sisters on a Jack Sprat spectrum of eating disorders, one anorexic, the other obese, scribbled in the paginated sidelines of *Essential Physics* by E. W. Rockswold. A niggling shame began coursing its way through her body, burrowing in deep like a chigger, down, down, down. Young finally looked her in the eye, then cast his gaze on the page, then on her again.

"Thank you," he said simply, pulling out a vast, world-building expanse of drafting paper. He drew her. It had taken all of five minutes, but when he finished, it felt like the first time, in a long while, that anyone had seen her, the real her. Not in the "you're pretty for a dark-skinned girl" or the "damn you tall, shorty" regard that made her feel like some gawky girl Groot.

Young found her lovely. He found her, like he had set sail that day and miraculously discovered her, landing wide-eyed and intrepid on uncharted shores.

That night she went home. Said the proper "yes, Mummys" at the dinner table and dutifully passed the *egusi* stew when prompted, all the while this new awareness surging inside like a secret superpower, tingling through her. She looked up sharply. Had her mother just given her a look from across the *gari*? She gulped the rest of her food as quietly as possible.

Later, in the dark of her room, she was glowing. A thousand Christmas lights flashing and manic, just under her skin. The sensation only just bearable. She knew how to be quiet about relieving the tension, no telltale rustling of bedsheets, no sighs—just a long pillow held tight between the soft V of her thighs, then a squeeze, a squeeze, a squeeze.

• • •

After way too many texts—*where u at? / getting sumthin 2 eat / by auditorium / naw, by Spidey statue / huh?*—Astrid finds Mimi in a clutch of adoring fans posing for photos. Mbola is ringside, holding Mimi's Fendi purse. Astrid supposes all the attention is partly in the novelty of Mimi as a "Black girl Psylocke," but most probably because her costume is basically a leotard and some strategically placed purple scarves that barely conceal her massive boobs. *Mammaries*, Astrid thinks. *Mammaries.*

Back home in Cameroon, some tribes *iron* girls' breasts when they develop too fast. Wooden pestles pounded *foufou* and flesh alike, anything that was sharp or unyielding would do really: a grinding stone, a coconut shell, a hammer held steady-handed over hot coals. Mothers beat down their daughters' breasts to keep them safe from come-too-quick womanhood, from the libidinous gazes of that older uncle, that schoolmaster, that strapping boy in the classroom's corner desk at their secondary school. Her mother was born of this tradition. Astrid sometimes caught her mother eyeing her long, wayward limbs in exasperation, as if her growth spurt was somehow a calculated rebellion. Astrid tries to be good, she does, but the harder she tries, the harder her mother becomes, still. Her sister Gwendolyn had tried to explain it once, stuff about Astrid being the "last cocoa," the late-life child their flagging mother tried doubly hard to keep in line, yada, yada, yada. It was all so exhausting—her mother's worries, her nameless fears—but Astrid supposed this was why her mother had lied about *The Photo.*

A week ago, Astrid had learned the truth, surrounded by dark *Twilight* poster boys vamping at her from the walls of Mimi's bedroom. She was checking her Insta page: scrolling past four "like" notifications and three new follows. Two were easily identified but the third was from some girl she vaguely felt she should know. Someone from summer camp, a Sugar Pine alum maybe? No, the girl listed her hometown as Bamenda, Cameroon. She almost asked her girls if they knew her, but they were busy: Mimi, supposedly studying but in actual truth DMing a Parisian bodybuilder on TikTok and a Filipino Tinderoni in BK; Mbola, checking out YouTube tutorials, how-to vids by Ms. D. Vine on the best way to install your own lace front. She looked at the girl's warm, glossy-lipped smile again and stopped cold. It was Adama. As in her cousin, Adama. Adama with 3,579 friends. Astrid had thirty-two. Adama in dozens of duck-faced selfies and ussies. Astrid had a grainy class photo as her profile pic. Wearing bifocals, no less. There were fabulous foodie flat lays. There was Adama with a braided fauxhawk, there with kinky twists, in an Escalade, in a Pajero, on a merry-go-round, *was that a jet?*, cozying up to a cleft-chinned guy tagged as Marcus Tambe, a barrel-chested footballer, a Marcus Konwifo, and a DJ Bae named Marcus Atekwana who looked like he used his washboard abs to scrub girls' panties. All the choice Marci.

Adama's life was amazing. *Verified.*

Astrid jumped up, stumbled to the bathroom, and promptly threw up.

How lame is my life? She dry-heaved once more. Twice more. *What life?* She wished she could facetune her whole existence, slap a Juno filter over it all.

Two days later she got her acceptance letter to Princeton, its words standing dark and ominous against the creamy paper. It was official. The reality of that almost made her throw up again. She felt ridiculous for dreaming beyond the picture-perfect life her family wanted for her: nice cars, nice houses, nice husbands, nice jobs. All so tidy. So prefab. Sometimes she went to the mall to get messy, to fuck things up. To pocket pens behind the cashier's back and fill that well inside herself. *Why? Why did she have to make such a fuss and want more?*

"Ouch. What the—?"

Someone just stepped on Astrid's big toe. Post-thirst-trap-photo-op, there is some slight jostling and jockeying for position among the tight band of young men—some spandexed, some not, some with eager lenses jutting, some with limp camera straps dangling and tangling as they press in close to her friend. Astrid moves back a bit and her sheathed *katana* pokes a guy in the belly.

"Sorry," she mumbles.

"No worries," he says, looking her over as he rubs his deflated paunch. "Who are you supposed to be?"

"I'm still trying to figure that one out," Astrid replies.

• • •

Astrid stares down at the NYC subway bench with its ritual scarifications, its palimpsest of celebrity memorials: *Tupac 4 Life, R.I.P. Biggie, Forever Whitney*. On their trek back to Jersey, Mbola and Astrid sit together silently for a number of reasons.

First, their mouths are full. Astrid is chewing wasabi nuts; Mbola is sucking on sunflower seeds, spitting their freshly desalinated husks in a long trail that makes Astrid think of children lost in fairy-tale woodlands.

Second, they are exhausted. The rest of the afternoon had surged forward in a blur: an advance screening of a new Marvelverse TV show, Mimi's "honorable mention" in a cosplay contest, and a pretty informative panel on how to survive the impending zombie apocalypse. While the "panelists"—three guys in fatigues toting Day-Glo orange rifles—handed out copies of an actual Centers for Disease Control zombie-preparedness guide, Mimi and Mbola argued survival scenarios, should an outbreak happen in Africa. Mimi figured high body counts: *They can't even cure Ebola, let alone some zombie virus*. Mbola was a tad more optimistic: *Stop playing. They would ether them zombie mofos. Them motherland Africans stay packing machetes*. Astrid tuned them out and took detailed notes for her lemony Richonne one-shots. She was big on research, had spent hours at the aquarium documenting all things piscine for her Afrocentric mermaid story, "La Sirène Africaine." Just then she was diligently recording instruction drills for how to kill or successfully elude the walking dead. Differentiating, of course, between Romero's slow, lurching *Dawn of the Dead* revenants and the quickened undead "zoombies" of *28 Days* and its ilk. Kill shots to the head were deemed universally appropriate.

Third, and most importantly, Astrid and Mbola are silent because they are alone. Mimi, their buffer, has decamped to a cousin's house in the Bronx, leaving them in one of those awkward moments when their simmering dislike—usually confined to the occasional whitehead flare-up—now took on a life of its own, gained sentience, planned world domination.

Mbola spit out another sunflower seed, breaking the silence, saying, "I read your stuff today. Y'all be killing folks all kind of ways—chopping off heads, shish-kebabbing eyeballs. It's mad dark."

"Yeah, that's Young's style," says Astrid. Young was crazy for chiaroscuro—all inky blacks, bone whites, with the occasional splash of red in a flagrant homage to his idol, Frank Miller. Her story lines fit the tone.

"You know just what his style is, don't chu?" Mbola says. "The way you be all up on him, all the time."

Astrid knows that Mbola is decidedly not Young's style. In a convo, months ago, he had dismissed the idea of dating her in less than a minute.

Mbola? I'd rather date a Japanese body pillow—better personality.

She's not all that bad.

She's hot but hella loud and—

Whatevs, date the pillow chick. I'm sure you and waifu, Keiko-tan, will have a real nice life together.

Damn straight. Once you go moe you never go back.

Mmmhmm. Better not honeymoon in Paris though.

Astrid had dropped an imaginary mic as she said this, then threw her hands in the air for that burn to end all burns. *Shinnichis* that they were, that Sunday night's viewing pleasure had been a documentary screening on the frequent mental breakdowns of Japanese tourists in the land of croissants and *vin rouge*.

All right, all right. I gotta give it up for a PBS snap, Young said, laughing. And Astrid didn't know what made her happier, his husky chuckle or hearing that he had no designs on her prettier friend.

• • •

"Astrid! You listening? You don't got nothing to say? You too good to talk to me now?" Rat-a-tat questions from Mbola, who was working herself into a state, firing up.

"No, I just—"

"Yes, you. You always looking at people and writin'. What you got in that pad about me? You know you ain't better than nobody. You ain't no hero."

"What are you talking about?"

"Talking 'bout you, bitch. You s'posed to be that blind ninja chick, Blue Ivy, Augur Blue—"

"Brown."

"Blue-black, doodoo brown, I don't care. You ain't her, you mad weak," says Mbola, stabbing a spiky acrylic talon at Astrid's face. "She can't see nothing but at least she open her damn mouth to talk. More than your ass can do."

"Get your finger out my face," Astrid claps back, refusing to step away, to cower, but then she falls silent. She always falls. The platform is hollow with her silence till the homeless man slumped over three benches away lets loose this klaxon of a fart. Till Astrid hears the muffled rumble of a train approaching on the opposite track.

Astrid is so not in the mood for this. It had been a long day of ups—she and Young selling half their stock—and downs—Baek Hyeon a no-show, sending an *Emergency at PG county shop. Rain check at MomoCon?* text. Astrid had felt a wave of self-pity (yet another holding pattern before her life could truly start) till Young cheered her up with a variety pack of her favorite Japanese Kit Kat flavors—matcha green tea, red beans, and soy sauce chocolate bars. Poking her in the back with one of his ubiquitous monogrammed pencils as he prodded. "And why are Kit Kats lucky, *senpai*?"

"Because their name sounds like *kitto katsu* in Japanese."

"Hmm. And what does *kitto katsu* mean, young grasshopper?" he said, stroking his chin's fill-in-the-dots stubble like a graybeard grandmaster.

His antics coaxed a reluctant smile from Astrid, quickly followed by a mandatory *this clown* eyeroll, as she mumbled, "You will always win."

"Come again? The Ancient One's hearing is not what it once was." He leaned closer, held his hand to an ear like the horn of an old-timey gramophone.

"It means: 'You will always win!'" Astrid yelled, garnering "Hell yeahs!" and "Hootie-hoos" from across the bustling hall.

That Kit Kat high and *hadouken* energy boost from Young's Mr. Miyagiesque pep talk lasted through the rest of the day but now her mind is full of worry on an empty platform, as Mbola rants ugly sometime-truths at her. *No more, no more, no more*, she thinks, feeling a pounding in her blood as the train, and Mbola, draw nearer. *No more!*

Astrid flashes to a vivid scene, another vision. Her *katana* slashes at air and sinew and bone. Blood blossoms from jagged platform cracks like vengeful roses. All that is left of Mbola, and her scorn, lies ruined at her feet. In her visions, Astrid is an avenger, fifty feet tall, fearless, *katana* in hand. Her voice a banshee scream, booming with conviction. She could be utterly herself, whatever her mind's eye imagines.

"Hey! I'm talking to you!" Mbola's strident voice zaps her back to reality.

"Yeah, get all quiet again, smart-girl," Mbola continues. "You so smart, why come you got to sneak out your house? Why you stay lying to your momz all the time?"

Mbola pushes her then. And for the first time in her life, Astrid pushes back.

She slaps, she jabs, she dodges Mbola's left hook. In their tussle, Mbola grabs her knapsack. Pulls away, panting and triumphant, holding it over the tracks.

"I'll drop it, bee-yatch," Mbola snarls through a bloodied, already swelling lip.

"Just try it," Astrid says, slowly unsheathing her *katana*. It's a dull replica really, but she knows if she puts enough force behind a blow, it will hurt like hell. Her mind fills with chiaroscuro, a darkness of slashing things: Mbola, Abel, her mother, and finally *The Photo*—nearly

bowling her over, nauseous with a need to hurt something. But then suddenly there is a lightness. She feels freed and filled with an awareness of her life beyond this moment, a future that is hers to choose, so she hopes. And there's that tingling again, the itching, sticky glow of it under her skin. She knows the truth of it now. Feels the zip of energy, the same zing up her spine after writing the perfect sentence. A power she has censored all her days.

Mojo, Astrid thinks. *Mojo.*

She lifts her chin high, lowering her sword to her side as she walks toward Mbola.

"Just try me," she says.

The Devil Is a Liar

Out of the mouth of babes and suckling infants, you have established strength because of your foes, to still the enemy and the avenger. —PSALM 8:2

There are hymns, there are hosannas, there are hallelujahs. There are some who are struck dumb in *His* presence and those who are newborn linguists—speaking in tongues. Eyes roll heavenward, limbs grow palsied, tears—of joy, of penitence, of defiance—are shed. Through this sound, this fury, Sister Glory Ngassa, Minister of Music for the New Africa International Church of the Holy Redeemer, Brooklyn Battalion, is praying fervently: *Thank you, Lord. Thank you, Alpha and Omega. Thank you, Oh Merciful One.* Glory glorifies and magnifies *THE ALMIGHTY* for the miracle he has wrought in the life of her daughter. Her voice, once whispery, rises, then rises again as she sways to the unsung chorus moving the faithful twenty-person flock present for service that Sunday morn. And faithful they are to the fledgling church—its sanctuary, a dusty Brooklyn apartment, a donated space, still undergoing a slow renovation that has spanned from Easter Sunday the year prior into an unknown future—unto the end of days, perhaps.

The congregation is sanguine in their shared burdens. Tried and tested; they will not be found lacking. So one had to watch one's step on the unfinished floorboards; a mere reminder that Jesus himself was a carpenter, a man who knew the grain of cedar, of poplar, of acacia, and even the bitterest wormwood. So the single-paned windows were unsealed and unshielded; their translucent tarp coverings fluttered in the draft like a host of angels' wings. Yes, the congregants of the New Africa International Church of the Holy Redeemer know they are blessed. Their leader, man of God, Pastor Godlove Akondeng, had journeyed all the way from church headquarters in Cameroon to share his special anointing.

Glory is bursting with a mighty testimony. Her daughter Temperance, whose belly had lain fallow for over a decade, is now with child. *Hallelujah!*

Three months ago, in this very church, the pastor had laid hands on her visiting daughter, covering her with the holy blood of Jesus. *Amen.* The two women's shared car ride to church had been one of quiet reflection, each woman siloed in sacrifice, contemplating the concessions they'd made to reach that moment. The mother remembered a month of cajoling her doubting Thomas daughter, weeks of *what harm would it do-es?* unanswered save for shrugging silence. The daughter remembered her husband's bedside homilies, her personal preacher man whispering *honor thy mothers* in her ear, his firm hands gently kneading her hips, the altar of the ironing board before them as she starched his clerical collars and Sunday bests. She had bowed her head and gritted her teeth in resignation.

Settled in together at the back of the sanctuary, mother and daughter waited as the service clocked in at two hours and twelve minutes: an abundance of songs and salutations, offerings and announcements, and a sermon so long-winded even the resolute wriggled impatiently against the unforgiving metal of their rented folding chairs. Then finally, the altar call, the open invitation to lay one's sorrows at the hallowed feet of the Lord. The main event to Glory's mind and many others if the throng of eager worshippers crammed in front of the makeshift pulpit was any indication. A platoon of Godlove's prayer warriors flanked the pastor as he moved through those gathered, their arms outstretched, ready to catch any and all poleaxed by the awesome power of the *Word*. That very moment, the good pastor was laying hands on the forehead of Brother William—felling all six feet of the man into the waiting arms of Sister Anna, raining down rapid-fire holy fire to break the ancestral curses that had kept the good brother from receiving his promotion, his increase. "Release him in the name of God the Father," he chanted. "Release him in the name of the Holy Spirit, release him, Jehovah-jireh; thy will be done."

Glory bowed her head, praying. Temperance bowed down low, re-adjusting the crumpled church flyer jammed under the foot of her wobbly chair. Feeling ill at ease as the ground shifted under her once again. Glory, even with eyes pressed shut in devotion, sensed her daughter's distress and reached out to squeeze her hand, willing faith and patience through her fingertips. *This was her doing, was it not?* Glory wondered. *What else had she expected?* All her life she had been a CEO—a "Christmas-Easter only" churchgoer playacting piousness. Her offspring had known nothing better. Now, she was determined to give her daughter the dose of belief she needed. Even if it went down bitter.

Glory stood up, pulling her daughter forward as the last stragglers freed the altar. She sucked her teeth as they passed Sister Matilda and Brother Ezekiel in the aisle. Unequally yoked, those two. The wife, crutching herself against the husband in deference to a newly acquired limp. The husband, clutching her piety to him like a security blanket, eyes darting, then downcast, seemingly abashed by the knowledge that Glory, and all those present, knew that he had hobbled his wife, disordered her steps.

At last Glory placed her daughter before her, offering her up to Pastor Godlove's waiting hands. Temperance tried not to roll her eyes as a man—*William, was it?*—jumped up to begin a jig of jubilation, before helpers whisked him away. Glory was appreciative. It was her daughter's turn and nothing would block her blessings. *Not today, Satan. Not today.* The man of God began to pray and the bliss of that moment, the brilliant relief of glimpsing a breakthrough yet to come, rocked Glory back on her heels. Even as Temperance stood stoic, Pastor Godlove's hands hovered over her flat belly, while he chanted *By the Spirit of Christ. By the Body of Christ. By the Blood of Christ* as he cast out the spirit of barrenness, beseeching the God of Abraham and Sarah, the promise keeper who blessed them with children as plentiful as stars in the night sky, to come into this place.

For years, Temperance had looked upon that same night sky and wept. But now, three months after Pastor Godlove's intercessions, Glory can testify on today, that joy truly comes with the morning. Her daughter had seen the signs and wonders for herself. *Hosanna in the highest!*

And now songs of praise and thanksgiving.

Glory steps forward. She pushes up her +1.5 drugstore reading glasses—perhaps it is time for +2?—and peers down at her hand-assembled hymnal. The photocopied fruit of her labors to harvest gospel songs from across the continent: Nigeria's Joe Praize, Cameroon's Tribute Sisters, the Soweto Gospel Choir.

"Jesus, we love you, Lord. *You don make my life betta. I go de thank you for evamore, thank you, Baba,*" sings the congregation, kept in time by the baton of Glory's pointer finger tap-tapping notes in the air. She is gratified. There is no instrumental accompaniment for this chorus of warbling voices—Sister Anna is always flat!—yet she knows to her marrow that their voices are pleasing to *He* who matters utmost.

Glory knows the power of church music. In over thirty years of searching for a church home she has been to many houses of worship and has come to know the quality of a church not by the size of the hats on the church ladies' heads or the crisp white gloves of its ushers. She knows a church by its music, by the way its people raise their voices in gratitude. *Praise Jesus!* She knows the Pentecostals love a good tambourine—a jangly rejoicing; Catholics crave a holy hush, hums of contemplation; while the Southern Baptists are ones for gamboling and holy rolling—lovers of big-voiced belters, soul claps, and organ riffs that settle on the sermons of their high-stepping reverends like a hype-man's cape across a shoulder blade.

For Glory, for *His* glory, the music has to be especially right this day. Her daughter is now over three months pregnant, well past those dangerous witching hours and months when a bumpy car ride could spell catastrophe. *Blessed be.*

Three months ago, the pastor had pulled Glory aside, spoke to her of serpents, of writhing knots in her daughter's insides, of the agent of the enemy who had tried to steal her dear child's womb, and the spiritual warfare he waged to protect it.

Later, she would tell her daughter of those snakes, those twisty fists pummeling her from within. "Oh, Mom," Temperance said, sighing. "I saw a specialist. Those were just fibroids."

• • •

Jesus, please Jesus, God, please, please, please. Let this baby be all right. This is the refrain in Temperance's head as she lies on the exam table, watching the ultrasound technician's wand stutter and stall—traversing ruts in the stretch-marked terrain of her mountainous belly. On the screen, her baby is airy and infinitesimal; a floating cumulous cloud. Yet there is a storm front across the tech's forehead, a worrying forecast, quickly gone as she shakes her head no to Temperance's question: "What's wrong?" She demurs, says, "We wait and see what doctor say," in a soft, lilting Russian accent at odds with her high-picked, Brighton Beach bouffant.

Please, tell me something, tell me anything.

"Tell me," Temperance says, grabbing the yolky, gel-soaked wand.

"I just technician. Doctor come soon. You know everything, in time."

The tech is out the door, leaving Temperance to berate herself. She could have been more persuasive, she just knows it. She could have displayed the oratorical prowess that holds all one hundred of her 1L students in thrall, even in that dogsbody of all law school classes, Professional Responsibility. She should have been serenely commanding, donned her First Lady mask, the one she used when she was spearheading the Marriage Ministry, Ladies Auxiliary, Bible School brunches, and Young Woman's Mentorship program at her husband's church. But she was too tired to be eloquent or uplifted. She is terrified, little else.

Something is beeping. She stares into the blank computer screen—the crèche that had cradled images of her baby. Another beep, near the sink, near the laminate countertop where a glove box bulges to bursting; syringes stab air; and a mad scientist's assortment of glass jars stand specimen-free. All feel menacing to her jumbled mind. There is another muffled beep before she remembers, exhales. It's just her cell phone. In her purse, hanging on a coat hook shaped like a stork's beak. Probably her husband, Andrew. Always so good about checking in even though he has no idea she is here. This visit is, and will be, her secret: too early to worry him, all too soon to weaken the faith of a jubilant congregation, four thousand strong.

Three months they had waited to announce the coming of this hard-won baby (conceived after no less than nine IVF treatments). Two Sundays ago, Andrew stood at the pulpit, she by his side, her hand practically crushed in his own as he spoke about the years of trying, about divine order, and the Lord's timetable. She was forty-two, having her first child, thinking *The Lord needs a new Rolex*. But that day, she smiled, and smiled. Strange hands reverently touched her belly each time she passed through the plush carpet corridors of the spiritual Disneyland that is their church campus. She smiled in the church gift shop as Andrew bought her an XXL maternity-wear "Jesus Saves" T-shirt and a copy of *The Christian Girl's Guide to Pregnancy*. She smiled when he reported an uptick in church revenue—offerings overflowing the collection plates, increased e-giving at the automatic tithing machines (ATMs). There was talk of renovations, a new annex, of recessed lighting. She smiled. Evidently, pregnancy was good business for the house of the Lord. Now this.

Another beep from her purse. She yanks her feet from the stirrups. Her papier-mâché gown bursts down the center, jagged edges scratching past her *linea nigra*, like a truculent piñata. She rushes to the phone to find solace in Andrew's voice, to drown herself in its deep end—so low, so sonorous. To let the soothing lap and cool lick of its sermonic undertones swell over her, as it did, even in bed, inside her again and again, making her scream his name, then *His* name. Preach.

"Andrew," she pants, out of breath from her scramble to the phone. "Andrew?"

"It's me."

It's only her mother.

• • •

Glory's spirit was troubled waters—churning, uneasy—till she picked up the phone to call her daughter. She had long ago learned, then forgotten, to trust that small voice of God within herself. It was the same voice that whispered to her fifty years ago as she lay sleeping soundly in her mother's hut on the night before she was to travel to America on scholarship for college. *Arise*, said the voice. She had tunneled deeper into her pallet and the warmth of her mother's arms. *Arise*, the voice commanded. She opened an eye in time to see a serpent slithering across the packed earth floor of her mother's hut. A sly, low-down dancer in the dirt. She screamed. Her mother had risen beside her, stepped on the snake, bashed its head in with the nearby pestle that had made a farewell meal earlier that evening. Her mother stood sentry, on guard the rest of the night. No serpents sent by venomous co-wives would keep her child from her breakthrough in a new promised land. That was a mother's love. That was the last time, for a long time, that Glory heard the voice—in the quiet of that hut, before the white noise and the din called America.

"It's me," she says again, voice high amid the clamor of Flatbush Avenue's weekend masses. "Is everything all right?"

There is a pause long enough to make her pull the phone from her ear and check its bars for reception. An artful dodger, she ducks past a man selling $1 subway swipes in front of the train station, past two women haggling over Gucci handbag knockoffs, into the quiet oasis of a small kiosk selling batteries, wristwatches, headphones, and incense.

"Temperance?" she says.

"Yes, Mother, what could be the matter?"

This is her daughter's legalese: answering a question with a question. Well, she knew her daughter long before the JD, when a stern look and the words *I'm disappointed in you* would send Temperance into tears. She tried again.

"*Apanga soh*, I have no idea what would be the matter. That is why I am asking." She tries her best to smile into her words, into the childhood nickname. "Eh, *apanga soh*. Tell your mama what's wrong."

"Mom . . ."

"Yes?"

"Nothing, it's nothing."

"You sound tired and stressed. Are you on your way to the church?" She glances down at her watch, then shoos away the vendor approaching her with wristwatch in hand. "Maybe you should skip the workshop. I'm sure they can spare you at least one day. School. Church. That crazy schedule of yours—"

"My schedule is fine, *Mother.*"

From Mom to Mother, almost as bad as the legalese.

"Besides," Temperance continues, "my firm has a generous benefit plan. I'll have plenty of time to rest on maternity leave after the baby is born."

"My grandbaby," Glory says, marveling how the words taste of sweet *koki* corn, cling like *eru* to her tongue. "Aren't you due for another checkup soon?"

"In two weeks."

"*Chey!* So long? I can come with you, if you like—"

"That's okay, Mom. Andrew has been coming."

Glory hears the sound of something ponderous, then Temperance falls silent. Then, finally: "Thank you, *Mom.* Thanks for checking in."

"Anytime, *apanga soh*, anytime."

After the call ends, Glory begins a catchall prayer, infused with every blessing she has ever wanted for her only living child. But above all, she hopes her prayers will fortify her too-strong daughter whose voice—muttering "goodbye"—had been so breathy and fragile, one of wind chimes forlorn and tinkling in an airless room.

• • •

Hours later, Temperance is leading a "Mommyhood: The Christian Way" workshop for unwed mothers. She takes deep breaths, still trying to channel her mother's certitude that this child was meant to be, ordained. The mothers around her are lollipop young, mainly from the projects, and chockablock with children. She can almost look at them now and not hurt. Before, her ovaries would ache just to be in this room with so many women who seemed to get pregnant if you so much as blew on them. Shanice begat Shanice Jr. begat Lativia begat LaRenée begat Jamelia begat Jameka. Begat, begetting, begotten.

Temperance had shared these thorny thoughts with Andrew once—confession, allegedly good for the soul and all. She had whispered that night, but her grievances somehow echoed in the cloistered silence of their bedroom. *Why, Andrew, why? Why would God bless them and not her? Hadn't she done everything right, everything expected? Waited to get her JD, her MRS. Why was she still waiting on her happily ever after?* Andrew knuckled tears from her cheeks, his eyes filled with such tender disappointment, as he reminded her she was better than that, a woman of God—above such petty, elitist notions. She bowed her head then. She listened as he prayed.

But sometimes, Lord. *Sometimes.*

The children are carousing in the nursery center with Sister Carol. Sister Angeline sits at the long meeting room table: assisting with welfare forms, extolling the virtues of the church's free day care for members, and handing out sullenly palmed pocket New Testaments to visitors. For so many of the women in this ministry, their Heavenly Father—God, Jehovah, Yahweh—is a Tyrone, a Segun, a Raul. Another deadbeat dad, noted only for *His* absence in their children's lives, for going down to that celestial corner store to buy cigarettes and never returning. They come for the food and for a few child-free moments. A state they believe is heaven, but Temperance knows can be purgatory. They usually come for her, for free family law counseling on navigating the court system for custody or getting that child support check. But today her line has whittled down, kindling-thin.

Ten minutes, done, up and stretching her legs; she walks over to one of the girls from the neighborhood. The one with a line in her name: La—a (pronounced LaDasha, she reminds herself), who is bending to peruse the low-lying wall shelf that houses their pregnancy and motherhood library, books on breast-feeding and babywearing, prenatal yoga and hypnobirthing. The girl's Dominican press'n'curl threatens to topple, doobie-wrapped high round her head in a ziggurat of hair, buttressed by spindly bobby pins. Two pins fall to the ground.

"Here you go." Temperance hands the girl her errant reinforcements.

"Thanks, Mrs. Pastor Ealy. First Lady." La—a's eyes are narrowed, swinging low to stare, glare it seems, at Temperance's belly.

Temperance had noticed the girl in the parking lot earlier: hip cocked to the side, neck swerving with bravado among her friends. She had seen the girl, yet only now, looking into the clenched, mistrustful face, did she actually recognize La—a. Or rather, she remembered that look. First seen last year on a Saturday afternoon in the clammy underbelly of summer. Evening newscasts had been rife with reports of the elderly and infirm falling prey to heat stroke in their homes. Senior living high rises turned mausoleums as forgotten grannies were found entombed, amid dust motes and lace doilies. In a mission of mercy, the church had opened its doors to the community, offering air-conditioned sanctuary from the asphalt wilderness beyond. The activity rooms had been teeming: throngs gathered around hospitality tables heaped with sweating Dixie cups of iced sweet tea. Name tag stickers affixed to their chests as eager church staffers enlisted them in various ministries. "La-ah," she said aloud to the young girl as she wrote on her clipboard.

"Naw," came the surly response. "You ain't saying it right."

Pen poised in the air, Temperance waited for the correct spelling. She'd heard them all in their diverse congregation: from Watermelondrea to Ireoluwasimikolakawe. The girl continued to glare.

"Here." Temperance handed off the pen and paper. Helpfully, she'd thought. "Feel free to fill out the rest of the form as you like."

The girl stared at the pen like it was a snake in the grass.

"I'll do it." Her companion, name-tagged Niecy, pushed forward to take the clipboard from her. "Already finished mine." Stabbing the pen nib into the intake form.

"Sadiddy bitch," they whispered as they sauntered off. It was only later that another church staffer, who headed up their GED program, clued her in. The girl was functionally illiterate, reading at the same fourth-grade level as B.J.—her ten-year-old son—now churched up and reading up, self-betterment for her babies.

• • •

Temperance leaves the motherhood library to find succor. Stealing away to a quiet Sunday school room. She dandles another woman's baby in the crook of her arm, fanning herself and the child with a Singles Ministry flyer. He fusses. She loosens the tight swaddle, freeing quilted bunnies to hop along patchwork furrows. The cottony hush is broken only by the thump of a small heartbeat as a peace like salvation comes upon her. Her eyes flutter shut. The confection-sugar lightness of baby powder fills her lungs as a tiny dimpled fist curls into the cotton of her sundress. She rocks. Back. Forward. Back. Forward.

The baby stirs. She dips her hand to his cheeks—soft and fluffy as chocolate pudding. She smiles at the pink, puckering O of his mouth rooting for mother's milk. A maternal song sweeps through her like a gospel, a revelation. In that instant, she knows what is required. This certainty she feels is familiar. It is what she sees in her mother's eyes even as she turns her own face away. She knows what must be done. Temperance casts a scant glance back at the barely open door. The quiet corridor beyond. On a sigh, she slips her breast free. Places a swelling nipple to the baby's eager suckle. Shudders with the rapturous joy of it. The rightness. She is replete.

The baby draws deep from the well of her again and again, but grows fretful. Whimpers at her dry teat. Teeth scrape tender skin. Temperance cries out. Recoils. Hands shaking as she soothes the child. Of a sudden, terror smites her. Nearly dropping her to her knees.

Good God, did I just? How could I? What if someone saw . . .

"Mrs. Ealy," a voice calls from the door.

She turns to face her judgment.

It's La—a once more.

But had she seen?

"My cousin Niecy told me you had Dante." The girl clambers over to her, arms crossed over a jutting, bullet-shaped belly. She stops short. Seems to sniff the air as she peers into Temperance's flushed face. Her eyes narrow.

"He-here," Temperance stutters. "He's all yours."

The girl is still and mute before glaring down at Temperance's stomach.

"Congratulations, *Mizzz* Temperance. Heard 'bout yo baby. Me, I got *three* kids," she says, placing a hand on her hip as she throws down the last bit like a mic at a rap battle, like she won something.

And Temperance supposes she has. In the fertility race she has ever been the tortoise to La—a's fast-tailed hare. She swallows. This tension she feels with La—a is familiar. It's the anger she sometimes inexplicably channels at her mother when life infuriates her. She smiles uncertainly, tries again to connect: "I know them. Dante, Michael Jr., and B.J., right?"

"Yup, all boys plus *this one*." She pats herself proudly. "Whatchu havin'?"

Boy. Girl. Andrew hadn't wanted to know either way. *As long as it's healthy*, he'd proclaimed, foiling her girlfriends' gleeful plans for a gender-reveal cake at her baby shower. A suspenseful knife slice away from that revelatory inner filling in pink or blue. But that morning, listening to Dr. Ravins's revelations: talk of *posterior nuchal skin folds* and *nonossified nasal bones*, of her *significant risk factor* age, then the faux hopefulness of *further testing* and *findings inconclusive*, after more blood draws and procedure scheduling, she needed an answer. She couldn't yet know if her baby had Down syndrome, so she had wanted to know something, one thing, for sure. Temperance hesitates, clears her throat.

"It's a boy," she says, out loud, for the first time, to anyone. Her chin lifts, her French-manicured hand is on her hip, now. "A boy."

● ● ●

"Good morning, Mrs. Ngassa," says Mary Teforlack, secretary of Staffing *Soul*utions, LLC, palming the mouth of a phone receiver like a psalter, whispering, "It's Marjorie, Marjorie Winstead on line one."

Glory sighs. Staffing issues at this hour? At 8:00 a.m., on a Monday. The Devil never rests. In her office the phone line blinks spasmodically. A thing possessed. But as she sets down the heft of her bag, shrugs out of her coat, and turns on her computer, she is thinking of another phone call, of her daughter, the cipher: full of secret compartments and neatly tucked-by thoughts.

Thirty-five years as a social worker. Fifteen as a small-business owner. She built this business from the ground up. It put her daughter through college. Through law school. Her nurses, her aides, their patients, their loved ones, all had come to rely on her, their rock of Gibraltar, their steadfast counselor. *Yes, let's revisit Mrs. Taylor's Pain Management Plan, she's definitely getting worse post-fall. Yes, your daughter's last days will be peaceful ones. At Staffing Soulutions, we pride ourselves in meeting our clients' physical and spiritual needs.*

Forty-two years a mother and she can't get her daughter to confide a thing.

Glory picks up the phone. Her best Peds nurse, Marjorie Winstead, is trying to "quit." In reality that means absconding with the lucrative Hallstead account: a Presbyterian family with two young boys, both suffering from Duchenne muscular dystrophy, both requiring long-term home care. Winstead speaks breezily of changing commitments and flex time, all the while holding the truth under her tongue like an SL tablet: *I am trying to steal your clients, Glory, to see them on the side for some tax-free money. It's been a great ten-year run, Glory, sorry about your commission.*

This is not going to happen. As Glory picks up the phone, scenarios—assignment roster shuffles, shift switches—scroll through her thoughts like images in a picture wheel. Click. Toggle. Click. *That case closer to Marjorie's daughters' day care is suddenly available, and wouldn't you know, it pays a bit more money, and sure, it's only a short-term rehab contract right now but the mother had personally assured her that she would need some help down the line. These things can be so overwhelming, you know how it is, Marjorie. You do, don't you? Thank you for your professionalism and dedication. Did I mention you were nominated for Nurse of the Year?*

Later that evening, in the sanctuary of her bedroom, she picks up a phone again. She calls her prayer line, gets a busy signal, calls again in five minutes, then ten. She is determined in a way that would have surprised her younger self. That young woman had never been particularly devout, had mouthed prayers mechanically during morning devotions at her all-girl secondary school. The young women of Saker Baptist College were groomed to be good, God-fearing girls. Their heavens-blue uniforms as prim as nuns' habits, their pleats as straight as church pews. They knew they were blessed. Glory had had her own truth. She knew if any blessings were to be had, they were those of education and access, the chance to learn "book" at the newly founded missionary school, one of only two that were educating girls back then. So when the missionaries came round to Kings' dorm to inspect their charges' trunks, she had no qualms about hiding her hellfire-red lipstick in a crooked wall crack. When they came to cut the girls' hair down to less sin-inspiring lengths, she tamped down her curls with coconut oil and water, till they got wise, began barbering with a scraping, toothsome comb and a ruler, measuring manes to within a millimeter of the scalp. Glory had always been a millimeter past defiant.

But things change. Life happened, she suspects. At age sixty-five, she knows there is much she had overcome: defied headmistresses who tried to steal her academic scholarship, survived what that Bafut man did to her in the bush, and learned to manage the rages of a once-mild husband, long dead now, who collapsed under the clawing misery of burying their only son.

She has always been a fighter, a woman who rose to her feet again after the TKO of losing a son and a husband. Yet she is older now, she is winded. In the final rounds of her life it feels good, feels right and righteous, to have Jesus as her cornerman.

• • •

They say some men are called to ministry. Others just went. The Called: men seized by a burning desire to serve, to fashion themselves into tools for *His* work, to be the balm that heals a wounded and bludgeoned world. The Others: their hubris, their showman's need to be spotlit, center stage wielding the *Word* to their liking. They preach a prosperity gospel, instruct eager congregants to sow to a prophet's rewards: their bank accounts, their homes, and their wives' baubles are sizeable, flush.

It is Sunday morning, mid-May. From the front row, center aisle, Temperance has a direct sight line to the pulpit. No obstructed-view seating for the First Lady—peering beyond *geles* and frou-frou fascinators. Temperance cannot hide. She fists her hands to mask their trembling in her lap, wincing as the sting of her wedding band's diamond cuts into her flesh—ungiving, millstone-heavy. Was her husband called or clay-footed? He had come to preaching later in life. I-banker turned self-taught theologian, a man whose authoritative messages bespoke insider dealings, a special in with the Lord. But was he called?

Praise dancers make calligraphic twirls in the air with a rainbow of arcing ribbons. The dreadlocked bass guitarist in the church's fifteen-man band strums a fevered rock rendition of a popular gospel number. Every man, woman, child, and even some of the seniors, in the thousand-person-capacity main sanctuary, are up on their feet singing with the Grammy-winning choir. Now, Andrew strides to the stage. All along her row, people ready pen and pencil to take notes in the two pages earmarked in the church bulletins. His special Mother's Day sermon is titled "A Worthy Woman." Parishioners scribbling furiously, as if prepping for a pop quiz by Saint Peter at the pearly gates.

Andrew reads from Proverbs 31, speaks of a mother's wisdom to her son, King Lemuel:

> *An excellent wife, who can find? Strength and dignity are her clothing, and she smiles at the future. She opens her mouth in wisdom, and the teaching of kindness is on her tongue. She looks well to the ways of her household, and does not eat the bread of idleness. Her children rise up and bless her; her husband also, and he praises her, saying: "Many daughters have done nobly, but you excel them all."*

He is moving, he is eloquent, he is looking right at her, this man, her husband. Any faith she has is secondhand, borrowed from him, now showing wear. Seams stressed by the tragedy gestating within her. She wants desperately to keep the faith.

Was he called?

If Pastor Godlove Akondeng and her mother are to be believed, not only was Andrew called, he was conjured. *Abracadabraed* into her life through holy hocus-pocus. Ten years ago, they had prayed and fasted for a week to banish the "spirit of spinsterhood" from her life. A week later, she met Andrew.

Was he called?

Please, Lord, let him be. Please.

Temperance needs the good Reverend Andrew Ealy Jr. to be called. To be a man who won't shun her for her doubts about caring for a special-needs child, nor rebuke her for mentioning the unmentionable: a termination. She needs a husband and a confessor, needs to be sure that all these years she has loved a man who can see his faithful, unflagging helpmate at her most helpless, and give her grace, still.

• • •

Her mother's home is mum, save for a duet of humming, one human, one mechanical. Low lullabies to a grandchild commingle with the dishwasher's contented whirring, purpose-driven, cleaning the dinnerware from their Mother's Day meal. Two greeting cards stand on the side table: one from Temperance, another on behalf of her brother, Caleb.

Temperance sighs as her mother rubs and rubs and rubs anointed oil into her skin, spiraling into the dip of her belly button. The circles are entrancing, Zen-pebbled perfection. She imagines her son—floating and free-diving inside her—must experience these soothing strokes like blips on sonar. She settles back into the sofa as her mother kneels before her, pouring holy salts, Godlove-blessed, in with the Epsom swirling in her foot soak. Bubbles play footsie with her squirming toes.

She braids her fingers with her mother's.

"Mom . . . I'm having a boy, a baby boy." She rushes to quell the wave of joy cresting over her mother's face. "But he might be sick."

"What do you mean, 'might be'?"

"Down syndrome. Maybe. Most likely." Temperance looks away from her mother. Guilt like a living thing inside her. If she were a worthy mother, possible birth defects would not sway her, she would fearlessly rise to the challenge—contacting specialists, researching cutting-edge educational opportunities for the developmentally disabled. She would thank God for this test of faith. Thank God for finally gifting her with the bundle of joy so many had kneeled and prayed for. Yet here she is. Wavering. Weak. She knew so many children who were challenged lived full and meaningful lives—that was the right thing to feel. It's the type of thing she would say counseling fretful mothers in her church. Being her best self, the kind of person who would shut down her friends' plans for a gender-reveal party because gender is a false construct and it's the child who chooses, isn't it? Values she thought she believed till she lost herself in the joy of imagining a boy who looked just like her husband. She looked back into her mother's searching gaze. "I'm going in for testing tomorrow, to be sure."

Her mother begins rubbing her belly again, raggedly now, halts, fingers interlocked, helmeting it protectively with her hands. She prays, goes quiet for a long moment, then asks, "What about Andrew. Have you told him? Does he know?"

"No. Not yet."

"Good. Don't. Nothing is certain."

"Are you telling me to lie to my husband?"

"I'm telling you to deal with it when the time comes. I'm telling you that men are not strong in the ways that we are. Look what happened to your father, when he lost *his* son."

"If something is wrong . . . if the baby is . . . affected . . ." Temperance looks away then, stares at her brother's card. Her eyes are wary and searching as she looks back down at her mother and says, "I'm thinking about having an abortion."

Temperance takes a breath. The air thick and close. An orphaned tub of shea butter pouts in oily abandonment, melting under a stained-glass lamp.

"All right," says her mother. "As long as you're sure, *apanga soh.*"

And she is stunned into silence. She had voiced the worst, expected judgment, imagined herself cast out of her childhood home, onto the concrete.

"Your grandmother, Mami Rebekah, had nine children, starting from the age of thirteen. Five died before they could crawl. Two before they could walk. Two lived to bury her. I had two myself. One lost to me all too soon. Nothing is certain."

Her mother's face looks soft, features fluffy with memory.

Temperance does her own remembering, of a tall, copper-skinned boy, a whirling dervish who swung her round and round till they fell to the ground laughing. She had wanted to name her son after this dizzying boy. Caleb.

"But you . . . your faith—"

"My faith is you, my daughter. You are a Ngassa woman. You will do what you must. And I will pray for covering as I stand by your side." Her mother stands. "I think I'll make you some of that special tea I bought you, the calming one. I will come with you tomorrow. But now, tea. Yes. Some tea."

The tea is raw and silken, larval. There was an echo of something in her mother's voice as she handed her the steaming cup. Something Temperance ponders after that first sip. She blows air kisses into its heat, remembering that voice slipping over when she was a child, plagued with bed-wetting night terrors till her mother tucked a dingy pouch under her pillow, just as she would a loosed tooth. Whatever it was, grains from the sandman's hourglass or goose feathers, she had slept soundly from then on.

Temperance sips the tea slow and sure.

Another sip, two, and she is filled with a warm lethargy. Teacup set aside, she lies down on the couch, nesting her head in the downy welcome of her mother's lap.

She wakes to weeping, a voice cracking on the lip of a sob as cleanly as an egg. Then other voices join it, praying feverishly, a sound like the roar of some great machine revving to life fills her ears. Drowsy, she moves to rise, and is gently pushed down.

"Mommy?"

"Shh, shh," coos her mother. "Hush, my baby. It's just Pastor and my prayer circle. See." Her head is palmed, positioned to see the assembled: a tall, oaken man; a squat, wobbly-voiced woman; and Pastor Godlove, who comes forward, still praying. He clinically examines her belly, still glistening slightly from its earlier basting, then extracts a small brass urn from his pocket. Dipped fingers emerge ancient and grayed; he paints ashen crosses onto her skin, the smell, singed and pungent. Temperance is volcanic, stomach queasy and churning for the first time in her pregnancy. *What is happening to me?* she wonders groggily. She braces herself, closing her eyes as another wave of nausea rolls over her. It passes.

There is a sound now of tender-footed elephants stampeding. Then the pastor's voice, exhorting the circle to trample the enemy:

"Let all demonic spirits troubling this baby scatter and die! Somersault and die! Die, die, die!"

Now, her mother above her, crying: "No weapon forged against me shall prosper! No weapon forged against my family shall prosper! We rebuke you, Satan. We rebuke you, deceiver. Liar. Deceiver. Liar. Liar."

The room grows hot. Temperance struggles to right herself, then feels silly, hormonal. She reminds herself she doesn't believe in any of this, does she? This, her mother's strange beliefs, an alien world of jujus and ancestral curses terraformed by Christianity. But maybe? For her baby? Just this once, she thinks, *this once*. She will let them finish their incantations, then she will get up, gather her belongings, and go home to face God, what little she knows of *Him*, on her own. She looks up at her mother's face, drenched in clean sweat and lamplight, about her a fearsome, soul-burnished glow.

Night Becomes Us

Night veils and reveals—her dark face tarted up with stars. Neon-lit. Flossing.

In alleys, on corners; users parlay with pushers. Johns politic with pimps, haggling for discount strange. Hip-hop and synth-pop coat the stained-glass windows of Cream, NYC's hottest new club—a deconsecrated church where bouncers in muscle tees play Saint Peter at the pearlies. Access granted. Or denied. Zeinab, the ladies' room attendant, sees none of this from her perch on a high stool in the bathroom—its inky, lacquered black licorice walls shine like mirrors, yet reflect nothing. But it is her job to see. To be ever vigilant in attending to others. She offers a paper napkin, then a shoulder to lean on, to a teary-eyed girl mumbling about that *motherfucker who thinks he's the shit, but he ain't shit.* The aforementioned *motherfucker* is in the VIP stash, blitzed on Ace of Spades, grinding on some shorty's phatty. At 3:00 a.m., he will wake up groggy, cuffed to a bedpost, wallet and Air King Rollie long gone, remembering his girlfriend—his ex now probably—had slapped him on the dance floor. Then stormed off to God knows where. *Christ.*

Zeinab is holding said girlfriend's hair back, a lace front weave unlacing in the steamy bathroom as the girl dry heaves into the sink. Preoccupied, she fails to see the woman in the purple-sequined mini stealing a fresh pack of spearmint and twenty-eight dollars of her hard-earned tips from the countertop. Her dream fund money.

Zeinab has purchased everything on offer herself: the candy and gum, mouthwash and mints, the combs, hair gels, scrunchies, safety pins, tampons, Band-Aids, Kleenex, lip gloss, snacks, stain sticks, a lint brush, aspirin, and antacids. Her tip jar is full to bursting with crumpled bills pulled from bras and teeny bedazzled clutches. She is well paid and well regarded for her insightful attentions: her crazy glue fix-its for broken stilettos, plastic slippers ready should the bootleg shoe surgery go bust. There is lotion on hand, redolent of water lilies and lemongrass. An appletini air freshener she spritzes in each stall. A crystal garden of fragrances: designer perfumes in vintage atomizers sourced at the variety store off the subway stop in her hood.

The first time she spritzed him with honeysuckle, her cousin's friend Sa'id told her that her name, Zeinab, meant "fragrant flower" in Arabic. This she already knew but she allowed him his moment, smiling sweetly, rewarded when he leaned into the crook of her neck—close yet not quite touching, an innocent, air *bisous-bisous*—inhaling deep. She laughed then, taking in his own scent—the honeysuckle, yes, but mixed with something native to him yet familiar, a heady musk that reminded her of evenings back home, lit by blazing stars and the blood orange embers of soft *sissoo* wood fires, burning bright. As a child, while her mother secreted away to their garden to ritually bathe her naked flesh in seasoned smoke, Zeinab dreamed of a different starlit haj, longing to steal away from home, cloak herself in men's garb, shadow the steps of her nomadic Bororo distant cousins as they tended *djafoun* cattle in the highlands. Roaming and untethered, whiffs of their scent on the wind were intoxicating.

"You smell like nighttime," she told Sa'id. "Like freedom."

"*Shukran*," he replied. "An *oudh* mixture my mother made before I came to America. 'Let it always remind you of home,' she told me. I dab it on my beard to remember where I come from."

Something ain't right. The tip jar looks off, looks light. Zeinab can tell, a neat trick she's picked up, like counting cards or all the jelly beans in a carnie's jar. Later, when it's quiet, she'll count to be sure—fanning *dollar-dollar* bills in her hands: some crisp, some faintly damp from their recent acquaintance with other skin, confirming what she already knows. She rifles through her memory for clues, sussing out the moment, the exact millisecond she got got. The culprit: Sequin Girl. *Wahala.* Her cousin Mamadou would be disappointed to learn she was robbed tonight, like some rank amateur. She was better than that. She knows to empty her tip jar, leaving just enough cash floating alluringly along its bottom, signaling to others that her services are worthy. Respected. When she arrived in the US six months ago, Mamadou had helped her land the attendant work. He was a washroom attendant at Silk, a Midtown gentleman's club, so he had schooled her on the ins and outs, even taught her the hierarchy of after-hours spots. To never work at a venue where grown-ups had to be told how to dress themselves. Who leaves their house wearing *salle caleçons, they filthy drawers dem*? The dress-to-impress codes: "No baggy jeans, athletic wear, Timbs, sneakers, fitteds, or T-shirts"—they were for lesser men, in his estimation. In fact, men in general were uncouth as far as he was concerned.

"Men. They no good," he told her in the broken English he insisted on speaking, en route to assimilation and his American dream. "Them pay big money for drink cognac and whiskey but them leave bathroom and no want wash their hands. Them take shit, spray cologne, then try for give you $1 with they dirty hands. Even asking for change. Disgusting! Save your shit for home. If you want shit give me $5. Piss for $3. Women are sweeter. Clean. So you no get for work so hard."

"We are not as sweet as you believe, my cousin." Zeinab spoke to her reflection in the empty bathroom.

After all, it was a woman who stole from her. Another whose umbrella-cocktail-steeped heartaches were a distraction, her downfall. She was too soft-hearted, too often fell under the trance of these ladies and their dramas. Each woman an urban Scheherazade, their tales enthralling. They showed up to show out, celebrating—a career break, a platinum-ringed wedding engagement—or mourning a breakup from that *emo, pussy-ass, fake-jack Drake,* or losing out on that *fucking* primo role they'd skipped two shifts at the café to audition for. Even their failures, even the way they said *fucking* fascinated her, speaking to their strength, their hot-blooded hustle. So Zeinab had listened and all the while her takings were taken! On a good night she could easily make $80–$100, money netted over hours on her feet serving as hand-maiden, therapist, beauty consultant, janitor, and, one night two weeks ago, as a referee when everything went flying, from accusations—*saw you scoping my man you trick-ass bitch*—to manicured talons: stiletto nails, bubble nails, furry nails, and acrylics. Zeinab had doused the catfight with water from her spray bottle, calling Big Tony from the front lounge to come eject the fight club wannabes. She worked hard for her money. No steady salary. Merely tips.

Now, she would have to braid two heads of hair this weekend to make up the shortfall. While her customers loved the elaborate poofs and plaited loops she had learned from her mother and Fulani tribes-women, she hated the ache in her fingers and back that lasted days there-after. Zeinab much preferred the work at the club. Its hours suited her well, allowing independence and an escape from the ever watchful eyes of her various aunties: from *Amma* Aissatou to *Khala* Djenabou. They had opposed her taking a job, but finances were grim and Mamadou—a more laissez-faire Muslim, fast and loose with his *salah* prayers and city-born in Maroua like herself—had insisted. Assuring them she would be well insulated, walled off even, from men and anything *zina.* Tucked by and by in a back room surrounded by women. He would be just across the hall, he said. She would be seen to, he assured them. Lies. Albeit necessary ones. Instead, he counted on Sa'id for some smidgen of truth, to sub in watching out for his little cousin a spell.

• • •

As she does each evening, Zeinab peeks out at the dance floor, peeps its spectral girls in body glitter shimmering under swirling strobe lights, shining. She smiles at the carefree creatures, unfazed by the hazy shroud creeping over the dance floor like the breath of some giant, slumbering juju. Earlier, while the DJ did his sound check—before the velvet ropes were lifted and the top-shelf liquor watered down—she danced alone in the bathroom, her own private disco. Her moves, her shimmy-shimmy-yas mimicked from vids online. Night becomes her. Every single inch of her body pulsating, pent-up cadences cracking open the yolk of her skin till something new emerges. She is a young girl—pure and unblemished, she is a young woman—gyrating, arms akimbo, knowing limbs vibrating with deep-welled wants; she is just starting to reconcile these dueling selves, because America is a place where one can be all things, all at once. All the way turnt up.

Now, with the short reprieve of an empty washroom, she closes her eyes, her heartbeat an 808 as she soaks in the music seeping through the walls, and loses all her selves.

"Nice moves."

Zeinab's eyes fly open. In the doorway, looking her over, is a speck of a girl in a lime green bandage dress plastered from breast to hip bones, what little there was of either. The girl's gaze was roving all over her, like she was hunting something to grab hold of, scoping a grip. This was the kind of round-the-way girl who stayed ready.

"You African?"

Zeinab looks at her reflection in the expansive wall mirror—brown girl, prim white dress. She wonders what gave her away. What else did this girl see?

"You is, ain't you?" the girl asks, her grin toothy and gold-plated as she moves closer. "It's all right, just asking. I come in here all the time and you so quiet. Real meek-like. But the way you was in here dancing. Shiiiiii-it." The girl winds her waist, twirling the bony baton of her pelvis in smooth arcs that somehow give her hips, her thighs more substance, conjuring curves where there had been none mere moments ago. Zeinab can't look away.

"I'm Temi." The girl extends a hand, brassy bangles stacked elbow deep, jangling and clashing together like toy tambourines.

It takes a beat or two before Zeinab thinks to extend her own hand, to offer up her own name in response. And when she does, Temi hoots triumphantly.

"See, see. I knew it. My pops was Nigerian. He dead though, so I ain't never been over there. But I can still always tell when somebody African."

Temi is jubilant, bouncing nearer, till she and Zeinab are toe to toe, and in spite of her four-inch Loubies, they are the same height, level. And close up, Temi's face, under a topcoat of foundation and fuchsia lipstick, is plump with the same baby fat as her own. All of this puts Zeinab at ease. The girl is way too young to be here legit, baby fat in Baby Phat. Big Tony had taught her all about fake IDs; he'd also taught her that knockoff shoes were just as useful as pat-downs and purse checks when assessing what he called "threat levels." Homies rocking greening gold chains and rhinestone Jesus pieces spelled danger, they came to the club ready to bust, thirsty for another man's swagger. These were the fools who'd walk up and straight sucker punch an NBA first-round draft pick out partying with his whole squad, then later, kicked to the curb from whence they came, would pop off rounds with a quickness. Bleached-blond sorority girls with cognac tastes on a coed budget, were known to appropriate neglected Chanel handbags strewn across leather banquettes. Big T and his security crew had a shorthand code; this type of patron was manageable with some occasional eyeballing: "Threat Level 2—Wangsters."

Temi was no threat, even though she was screeching at the moment.

"Ow, ow, ow, ow. You got a Band-Aid or something? Messed around and forgot what I came in here for. This redbone chick just burnt the fuck out my arm. She claimed it was an 'accident' but I saw her eyeing my shoes. Just hating. They real red bottoms, you know. Girl, I was about to pop off. She lucky I'm trying to be good tonight though."

"Why?"

"Huh?"

"Why are you trying to be good?" Zeinab is truly curious. All her life she had tried to be good—study hard, pray faithfully, be of help to her mother at home. She'd believed this righteous path was a ward against the world. But it wasn't.

Temi takes her time answering, helps herself to a complimentary Tootsie Pop, sucking contemplatively before finally she says, "I'm just trying to do better. For me. For my man. Wilding out gets tired. See this burn right here?"—she extends her unbangled arm—"I'm going to put some Vaseline on it, keep from picking at it, getting it aggravated, and it'll be like it never happened. No scar. Nothing. Sometimes things just need time to heal."

She puts her hand on Zeinab's shoulder. Smiles.

"Now show me that dance."

In the early hours of the day, Zeinab packs her countertop wares into four bins and a laundry cart, then goes outside to sit on a hydrant near Sa'id's cart.

"*Shukran*," she says as he hands her breakfast—a halal chicken gyro, generously drenched in white sauce, a creamy goo bubbling through her fingers. Meat cooked to perfection on a hot plate. They break night chatting as she awaits her cousin Mamadou's arrival for the daily ride back to the Bronx in his beat-up Dodge Diplomat. Sa'id often grew expansive in the pink flush of the predawn hours, teaching her Egyptian slang—*you are a* muza, *a beautiful girl,* "hot"—and some Arabic phrases to flesh out her slender vocabulary of Qur'anic verses and *hadiths*. Back home, her Fula mother had spoken Fulfulde. Her Christian dad had spoken French and Bamilike and at least twelve other dialects helpful in selling his leatherwork at the Maroua marketplace, yet had barely spoken to her at all since her mother died. But Zeinab refused to speak on such sad things at sunup, refused to tinge the day's possibilities with sorrow. Instead, she listened as Sa'id, who told her his own name meant "happy," spoke excitedly of his grand plans. Of how he would become a BIG MAN, *insha'Allah*. Saving up seventeen thousand dollars for a black market permit from Habib Hamini—a distant uncle who had waited ten years for his own permit, and since retired to Sharm el-Sheikh, living large from renting his much-coveted, limited-supply, two-hundred-dollar city vending-cart license. Every night at 3:00 a.m., Sa'id pushed his shiny silver cart to the front of the club to catch the flow of clubgoers tottering down its marble steps—tipsy and ravenous.

• • •

Nighttime is full of deceptions, of temptations, of taboos. Its allures almost always *haram*.

Nighttime is for spirits and libations. *Haram*.

Nighttime is for touching the curve of your lover's shoulders. *Haram*.

Back in Cameroon there were curfews for the nighttime, cautionary tales of headstrong girls who had followed the wrong men into the darkness. But your anxious schoolteachers, and aunties, and the errant shopkeeper never warned you of the dangers lurking in broad daylight.

On a bright sunny day, holding her mother's hand as they bought food to celebrate her sixteenth birthday, Zeinab and her mother, Mariama, were blown up. A sixteen-year-old girl named Hanifa detonated a suicide bomb not ten yards from where they stood buying tomatoes. Mariama was thinking of her husband's dinner, she was humming a pop song her daughter teased her for knowing, while examining sun-ripened tomatoes, some pocked with black carbuncles. Her daughter's hip bumped the table, toppling a cavalcade of red that went rolling and rolling in the dust till hitting the knees of a girl, about her daughter's age, kneeling in the dirt. The girl's hijab had fallen back from her face to reveal a head of unkempt and uneven cornrowed hair. Mariama clucked her tongue in sympathy. Her last thoughts—before she saw what was cradled in the girl's lap, before comprehension curdled a scream in the base of her throat—she thought to herself, *Where is that poor child's mother?*

• • •

Hanifa adjusted her hijab. She wanted to be beautiful and most worthy in *His* eyes. She had walked right to the center of Maroua Marché Centrale just as the Commander had instructed. The kneeling was her own design. She would enter the afterlife in supplication. Al-Quddus would be merciful. Eleven months prior, she was kidnapped from a village schoolyard by a band of jihadis self-styled as the Islamic State's West Africa Province or ISWAP or Boko Haram or better known still by the people as the devils terrorizing the Far North region. Hanifa was a slave, used by everyone, till the Commander made her his bride. Nine months ago, she fled in the night as the group decamped from the caves of the Mandara Mountains to their lean-tos in the Sambisa Forest. She ran miles home to a village whose people rebuffed her. Who gnashed teeth and shook heads in suspicion as she came by. So when she felt the woman pains and saw her belly growing round with the Commander's seed, she returned to her husband. Told him she would be a soldier in Allah's army, but told him nothing of the child. She hoped her son, she knew it was a boy, would have a better life in the next world. She clasped her hands together, to Christian onlookers she seemed to be in prayer, yet in that simple act two wires touched, completing a blast connection that left thirty-five bloodied in the dust and the charred bodies of eighteen victims, including her own.

• • •

Zeinab flew up in the air as the shock wave hit. Before pain, a nanosecond really, she thought she might take flight. Lifting up and up and up. But then pressure came over her. A concrete wall collapsing. Falling from grace to the ground. Then her death for two minutes and her mother's for an eternity. Zeinab came to in a world transformed. White dust on ripped clothing, in hair, in throats. Screams. Carts charred and overturned. Bodies bobbing in the dirt—face down or belly up, sightless eyes fixed on the fractured skyline. Torn bits—of flesh, bone, fabric—scattered everywhere. A father wailing over his wife and child. Over her.

That first month after, she spent at home, healing her soul. The second month, her unassuming father, a man whose leatherworking made beautiful the remnants of dead things, joined men armed with machetes and arrows and bush rifles, a self-defense militia standing ready to pick up where the government's Third Bataillon d'Intervention Rapide left off. The third month after, the whispers began about a girl who had lived when so many had died. A girl with *gris-gris* who emerged, body healthy and seemingly unscathed. In the Maroua market people rebuffed her. They gnashed teeth and shook heads in suspicion as she came by. When she came home at night, her father held her tight, thinking how much she looked like her mother, unable to live with a ghost. He went off with the others to patrol in the dark. Left Zeinab standing alone wondering why her father looked right through her, wondering had she died in the marketplace too.

In the fifth month after, another bomb detonated. Another village. Another girl.

By the sixth month after, she was on a plane, passport stamped with an asylum visa, on her way to a place in America called the Grand Concourse. The plane lifting up and up and up.

• • •

"Do you think one who never sleeps can still dream?"

When Zeinab asked him, without thinking Sa'id said yes.

He believed in the American dream, in rags to riches and VIP stashes. In flossing. He was a striver like his elder brother, Tariq, and their father before them. Ready to fight so that Egypt could be prosperous once more. He and his brother were at Tahrir Square with their fists raised on January 25. They organized, mobilized, marched, got gassed and bled in the streets. Even as the government tried to shield its mess from the judging eyes of the world, suspending mobile service, even shutting down the internet itself, they protested louder. The revolution would go on. So strong was the people's voice that it only took eighteen days to topple Mubarak's thirty-year regime of corruption and injustice. But by then hundreds had died. Many were injured, including his brother. But still they were hopeful. But then came the Muslim Brotherhood with their own brand of repression. The weakening economy. His crippled brother left with no work. Left him wondering at night what they all had fought for. His uncle Habib had offered a lifeline. His mother told him to take it. He came to America with a bitter heart. His hopes like ashes in his throat. Then a sweet girl spritzed him with honeysuckle. A girl whose world was blown apart and miraculously she survived. If she could rise from the ashes, maybe he could too.

• • •

"It was only ten dollars," Zeinab lies evenly (she always downplays her earnings) as she hands Mamadou his cut, what he called his finder's fee. He *had been* disappointed to learn she was robbed like some rank amateur. *Did I not teach you better?* he asked.

"Here," she rolls her eyes sideways as she has seen American club girls do. "You still have forty dollars. And yes, I will do better tomorrow."

It's 4:00 a.m. and Mamadou is behind the wheel, the big boat of a car bouncing on the concrete waves of the Grand Concourse. He coasts, dreaming of upgrading to a new used car so after his night shifts he can make Uber pickups in a better part of town, can make more money to send home for his wife. In a month, in a rare show of softness, he will confide this dream to Zeinab, who will take pity and give him a bigger nightly cut, but for now she gives him *"side-eye, is it?"* and keeps stockpiling funds so that the very next spring will find her breathless and twirling in a modern dance class at a Harlem studio.

"Cousin. Did I not tell you no trust women? They dancing all night with *different-different* man. Who can trust them?"

"Yes, cousin."

"You keep your eyes open all times."

"Yes, cousin."

"'Yes, cousin. Yes, cousin.' I know you are city girl. I know you say yes to me in day and no in the night. Is okay. Your mother make you good girl." He had a habit of changing the subject whenever talk turned to his favorite aunt. But today, he lingers.

"You know your mother give me money to come to America. She do hair braiding for tourists because I no have a good father. She take care of me. Like I do for you."

Hearing her sniffle, he turns, asking, "Zeinab, why you crying?"

"No, cousin," she says, lifting her face. "I'm laughing you see."

Earlier that morning, talk with Sa'id had also turned to mothers.

"You taste the difference, no?" he had asked. "Fresh *dukkha* spice. Sent straight from home by my mother. Look, she even sent photos of her and Tariq." He felt slightly chagrined handing over old-school print photos. "My *umma*, Barak Allah Feha, doesn't believe in digital. She won't even email and . . . Zeinab *habibti*. Why are you crying?" But even as he asked her, he was already berating himself, knowing her thoughts must have flown to her own family.

"Come on now. This food is too good for crying. This day's too young. And this song," turning up the Sufi rock on his radio, "this song is my jam, it's made for dancing."

Then he was clapping. And hopping. And pulling her up from her perch on the hydrant.

"Sa'id, no! We're outside. The people. Everyone will see and—"

"Let them see," he said, doing a ridiculous whirl-push-shuffle step that made her laugh till she had to hold her belly. "I got this."

"You call that dancing," she said on a twirl. "I'll show you dancing."

She moved like she was seeking a spotlight. She shook and shrugged her body free of all the world around her. And it's like moon time in their garden back home, her father's weathered hands on her mother's waist, holding her aloft, twirling. The scent of mother's smoked skin perfuming the air. Red dust slippered her father's feet. Both of them giddy with dance, with the tinny rhythms of Sufi rock and *makossa* wafting from the radio. And a man with a voice like warm sugarcane holds a tremulous note so high and true it takes to the stars. Steady and soaring. Lifting up and up and up.

Schoolyard Cannibal

Youth makes you too apt a pupil of coarse lessons it takes decades to unlearn. Your headmistress, a family television—ancient, venerable—cased in oak heavy and vast as the *Encyclopedia Britannica*, entire. Poor, poor pickaninny, pick a program. Poison. Drink in definitions as you sit transfixed on grainy carpet, chin on the kickstand of your knuckles. In looney toons, you are jungle bunny—drum-bottomed, tuber-lipped. You coon for that rascally rabbit. Savage beneath ivory smiles. In sepia broadcasts, you are darkie, cowering to a towering Tarzan—a broad-framed, onetime Olympian, swooping down from

treetop fiefdoms to be your savior, your civilizer. There is a peculiar lull as your agile young mind absorbs these images, so at odds with those of parents and uncles and aunties cum doctors and lawyers and engineers. A chimpanzee familiar is smarter than them all—these spearchuckers, these cannibals. A cruel tutelage.

You were once a Brownie. Awarded a Wilderness Survival Patch for handily identifying which innocuous sparkle-veined leaf inflames, itch licking skin, given the slightest brush. But the school playground at recess is a curious kind of badlands of concrete-sunk jungle gyms— its wild ones wear high-tops and Kangols, have brown faces that are cousin to your own yet claim no kinship. They hoot hot and holler. Their tongues tinted—purple or blue or yellowed from time-stamped taffies—lash out. "African booty scratcher. Betchu live in a tree. Bet yo' mama's a monkey." You try for calm, take big, gulping breaths that puff up your lungs with air gone to rot. But you are swinging now, punches wild, child, some landing, some not.

Later, hurting in places unknown, you ask your family *Why do they hate me?* and *What about me is wrong?* Your father, who is a professor of cultural anthropology, will try for social context, speak of old wounds. Of wires-crossed associations linking you with treacherous tribesmen who sold off their enchained ancestors to slavers dotting Cameroon's coast. Your Uncle Elias, who drives a gypsy cab and has no papers, will tell you to ignore the ignoramuses: "Eh-eh. These *akatas* barely go to school, even though it is free. Me, I have a whole master's degree and cannot get work. *Nyamangoros!* You are better than them. Who cares what they say?" Your Aunty Alexis, who bleaches her skin and married a very fat yet very rich *mukara* man, tells you Africa is doomed. "We could be strong; but we never unite like the whites. Our rubbish leaders sell our countries, our futures, for *dix-dix* francs. Your schoolmates were born in America. Who wants to be African?" Your mother, who is a psychotherapist and a prolific hugger, will tell you it is because they are yearning, learning late to love themselves, still so mired in their pocked history. You remind them of all they have lost.

Your fourth-grade homeroom conducts safety drills. Students orderly file out from class imagining infernos at their heels or practice futilely ducking beneath desks in the event the Soviets should do the unthinkable. Your teacher, Ms. Bunches—she of the closed-book pop quiz and nightly essay assignment—performs spot hygiene checks after roll call. They say she can smell nasty at thirty paces. You watch her face for signs. For a telltale twitch of her high, pinched nose. But there is no emergency alert system. This is not a drill. She sidles up to student desks, ostensibly collecting homework, pausing, sniffing out the secret stink that had beckoned her from her blackboard. Flop sweat beads, then trickles down your back. She is behind you now. You clamp down your arms. All too late. "Raise them," she says, head bent to yours. A chalky stick of deodorant materializes, flaking white like her hair. "You need this," she whispers. "You've got the African smell." Head bowed, you let her mark you; never quite sure what she means by "African smell" but somehow knowing it reeks of dank humiliations and day-old bologna, moldering.

> *AxeSureSecretOutlastRightGuardAxeSureSecretOutlast*
> *RightGuardArm&HammerAxeSureSecretOutlastRight*
> *GuardAxeSureSecretOutlastRightGuardArm&Hammer*
> *AxeSureSecretOutlastRightGuardAxeSureSecretOutlast*
> *RightGuardArm&HammerAxeSureSecretOutlastRight*
> *GuardAxeSureSecretOutlastRightGuardArm&Hammer*
> *AxeSureSecretOutlastRightGuardAxeSureSecretOutlast*
> *RightGuardArm&HammerAxeSureSecretOutlastRight*
> *GuardAxeSureSecretOutlastRightGuardArm&Hammer*
> *AxeSureSecretOutlastRightGuardAxeSureSecretOutlast*
> *ProtectProtectProtectProtectProtectProtectProtectProtect*

Another February. Your homeroom plastered with posters on BLACK ACHIEVEMENT—all caps imperative. Inventors and innovators who gave us pencil sharpeners and peanut butter, blood banks and traffic signals, street sweepers and dustpans. But something is new this year: portraits of African royals from antiquity, graciously supplied by a prominent brewery. King Tenkamenin of Ghana; Makeda, queen of Sheba; Emperor Mansa Kankan Musa of Mali; Queen Nzingha of Matamba; King Shamba Bolongongo of Congo. A bevy of tongue-numbing names like your own to be memorized along with the liturgy of Charles Drews, Garrett Morgans, Ida B. Wellses, and Mary McLeod Bethunes. Eyes unblinkered, your classmates look at you anew. Something like pride seizes you. You're shook. But memories are short and March rolls in. The continent is on the news once more, embroiled in another far-flung war. Lenses zoom in on HD atrocities in the here and now. Black History. Black Present.

In grade school, you know that you are smart but never pretty. There are always more obvious contenders: Taniesha, pussy-eyed with long, Cherokee-blood good hair; Kiesha, who let DeVante peek at her panty-drawers behind the slides. Rom-com dream girls never look like you. Then there is a PBS series starring you or at least your distant relations. Beautiful Zulu queens: courtly, coveted.

Your parents let you break night for "educational viewing" as you are their *Gifted and Talented* child—a blue-ribboner in *Olympics of the Mind*. You fall asleep on the couch dreaming. The next school day, boys froth with talk of Zulu girls and their Hottentot teats (bared by the SABC, for historical accuracy). *Yo, you see that redbone with the bee stings? You see that* mami *with the milk jugs swangin' like um-dada-um-da. Titties. Tetas.* African *tatas.* Heads swivel. Eyes zoom in on your frame. It's shocking being seen all at once, by so many. You flush. Crossed arms cover what has yet to develop. For years, while Taniesha gets hickeys at the back of the bus, while Kiesha gets a baby bump, you get As and Bs but no kiss after prom. For you are African, and by this culture's definitions, unsightly.

An Admissions counselor at your dream college speaks of wondrous opportunities. She leans in to share a moment with you, future Ivy Leaguer. "Your kind does so well here," she murmurs, adding confidentially, "not like those *others*." Her smile is knowing. So you smile back. Are you smiling in agreement? In gratitude? Because those who once hurt you are now made small? You're undecided. But it's not like the moment will stand isolated. Its twin comes as an African American financial aid officer frowns down at your application, tells you "you people" are why her son can't go to college. She stamps an angry approval on your paperwork. So you smile. Are you smiling in agreement? In gratitude? Her colleague pulls you aside, tells you, "Chile, she just mad her son got caught up in these streets." You smile. But sometimes, in the sullen dark of your dorm room, you remember and only then and just then and finally then your throat constricts, your face too tight for smiles, vise-like.

College tests you. There are Swahili 101 electives, classmates in Bantu knots, and kumbaya African Student Union meetings, monthly. *Yes!* Yet certain lessons are trying. A media studies class schools you on *symbolic annihilation*—the omission, the mis- or underrepresentation of whole peoples in book leaves, in film reels. And you remember your skin is the color of redaction. You remember confusion as old elementary school "friends" poke you online. Who are they? Their names are never next to yours in class photos, in yearbooks. Were you friends? Where is the evidence, the proof of life? Hives punch through your skin like pissy ellipses. Scratch them raw till a patient school therapist explains that *this* is how a body purges upset. No matter how long suppressed.

Try and try to forget. Your memory had always been fuzzy, tending toward breaks in the transmission, bald spots of time you had jokingly dubbed "selective amnesia." But still moments remain. You, ittybitty—all nappy plaits and teddy bear eyes. A soft one you were. Keen on gold stars. Undone by scolding. When you made mistakes—as children are wont to do—there were inconsolable fits of despair. Your worried mother gifted you a children's book on self-esteem whose pages held a mirror. She bid you look. Singsonging of all the ways in which you were wonderful. *You are smart. You are beautiful. You are worthy. You are kind.* Your agile young mind struggled to absorb those images, so at odds with those of books and television, of schoolmates and teachers alike. The mirrored book grasped tight in your trusting hands. *Look again, child.* Mama told you. *Look.* But you were gum-drop young: tender-headed and tenderhearted. You turned from your likeness.

It Just Kills You Inside

(Based on True Events)

Boogeymen are real in Africa, folks. Both the real ones and the sticky crude imaginings that ooze up from the darkest of hearts. They are gold-epauletted military despots who disappear your loved ones in that bump of the night. Or Big Pharma execs donating untried and untrue drugs to guinea pig villagers for tax write-offs. And then there are the workaday nightmares that complicate waking life, come courtesy of the tribalist, the spiritualist, the herbalist. This is why the first reports were dismissed as so much hinterland superstition, bush whispers in the dusk. This was Africa after all—the land of juju, obeah, and kamuti. A place where death rides in from the desert on horseback.

With all these familiar horrors, who in the hell was going to believe in zombies?

No one, for a very long while, when yours truly was on the job. You see, tropical governments hire outfits like mine for their cover-ups. I am what some might call a "fixer." My specialty: crisis management and communications—coming in after that burst oil pipeline wrecked the endangered ecosystem of some tree hugger's wet dreams or after your company's homicidal aspirin spree-killed dozens, tamper-proof seals about as secure as a buck-toothed virgin on prom night. I'm the man who got that sensitive CEO in front of the cameras, contrite and doling out "heartfelt" assurances about *maximizing safety measures* and *thorough reexaminations of system protocols*. Even better, I trained him to cry on cue—one muscular, robust tear, of course, all manly like.

There was a lot at stake back then: a good name, millions in foreign currency, political capital worth its weight in bullion. What was a few hundred thou between my kleptocrat buddies and me for a tidy little media campaign that whitewashed the first zombie death tolls? I'd said yes before I even believed them. So used to the garden variety brushfires of their regimes—political purges, coups d'état, ethnic cleansings—that I all too easily dismissed the Z word as complete crapola.

Were they really trying to bullshit a bullshitter? Don't piss on my leg and tell me it's raining. Insulted, I hiked up my retainer. Resolved to get to the what's what of things when I got to ground zero in Cameroon.

• • •

Twenty-odd years ago, in the badlands and bedlam days, French scientists had been flown into Cameroon on the hush for research support. Their government always did take a special, mostly mercenary, shine to their former colonies. The country was one of several puppet regimes they propped up in the region. I was flown in to whittle down their science jargon into reassuring sound-bite-sized pieces and forestall any community hissy fits with PR pabulum.

There had been a lab-coated Frenchman, a Dr. Georges Orliac, a head honcho at the European Centre for Disease Prevention and Control, Paris offices. He was flanked by a retinue of bespectacled suits and coats, quickly introduced, quickly forgotten, all looking at me expectantly. But first they gave me some papers to sign, "eyes only, confidential" type stuff. Standard for most of my clientele but somehow there seemed to be more emphasis on this ink, more jittery eye-balling of this particular John Hancock.

"You know about Lake Nyos, *Monsieur* Connor?" Orliac was fidgeting with his glasses.

"'Course," I said. "Summer of '86. Nearly two thousand dead. Natural disaster, bucolic lake goes acidic, belches up a cloud of CO_2 gas that asphyxiates villagers for miles 'round. Takes out their livestock, too."

"*Oui, oui.* And about the Israelis?"

Yeah, I had heard, rumors of secret Yehuda bomb sites, conspiracy theories that confounded even me, King of Misinformation. A lake goes kaboom and suddenly it's an international plot; talk of government payoffs allowing nuclear tests in subterranean lairs was bolstered by the Israeli prime minister's immediate in-country presence, swooping in with a fully equipped hospital plane just days after the disaster.

"I know some," I replied. In my business, information sharing was a game of hide-and-seek or keep-away.

"The rumors are true," he said. "The Israeli military was testing a neutron bomb; that is what detonated the gas."

I was quiet a spell, studying on it. I'd heard my own rumors. More likely, the French had done this themselves, broken a beaker or two of something heinous, and now were on to the slapdash ass-covering phase of the project. Either way, I was on the job. Orliac thrust a stack of photos at me—exhibit As and Bs and such.

"What you are looking at are the villages of Sobum, Chah, Koshing, and Nyos," he said. "Fertile lands, barren now. We have been studying and treating the survivors of the disaster . . . getting the usual complaints: heartburn, lesions, and neurological problems like monoplegia, forgive me, muscle paralysis to one part of the body. You follow?"

I nodded. "This is all well and good, Doc, but why am I here? Nyos was in '86, five years ago, ancient history."

"You are here because there were other survivors besides the living." He searched my face for some reassurance that he should proceed. "The dead, those who succumbed to the initial gas cloud—some buried, then some, some we kept, set aside for study—they rose."

They rose? They resurrected? Yeah, right. Was he really trying to bullshit a bullshitter?

I was in his face then. Giving him a shake. Mussing up his crisp lapels. "That's the craziest thing I ever laid ears on, Doc."

He was rattled, then he rallied. His fervent gaze settling on me with all the might and will and smiting force of a true believer. Doubting Thomas that I was, I couldn't quite put my faith in the good doctor's pronouncements. I was a practical man who needed hard facts and real-world answers—not hokum, not hoodoo. I wanted out of that peculiar revival tent, was walking out of the room when the doctor said, "Look." That was all he said.

Four minutes later, I did. Got blue in the face.

"Christ-al-mighty," I whispered, then loudly, "what the hell have you boys gone and done?"

● ● ●

"Une autre tasse de café, monsieur?"

I wake slow. See the dishy Camair stewardess, hovering. More than two decades after the first outbreak, here I was on a rusty tugboat of a plane headed back to Cameroon, the first hot zone. The plane shimmies. She rolls, then rights herself: *"Café? Thé? Chocolat?"*

"Oui, un serré," I answer. Struck by a powerful need for strong brew and a cigarette and maybe a shave.

We hit a patch of turbulence that tosses me about like Sunday wash. I'm getting too old for this shit. My churning gut nothing to do with the gore-filled pictures on my lap. Pain from the old bite flares up alongside my right palm, insistently, forgetting that there's no hand there to speak of. Shuffled photos drop to the cabin floor and I catch maybe one, maybe two; still a piss-poor southpaw all these years later.

"Ah, je suis desolée," says the stewardess. She is pushing one of those spit-shined meal carts, its wheels steamrolling the more adventure-some photos that have bushwhacked into the aisle from a thicket of armrests and collapsible trays.

She stoops to pick up wayward snapshots, underfoot and under wheel, then gasps, exclaims, *"Mon Dieu, mon Dieu, mon Dieu—"*

"*Ils sont faux, pour le cinéma*," I lie, thrust the glossies into a waiting folio, but it's too late. I know that look. She goes all still then shivery on me, her eyes the glass of high-rise windows reflecting nothing but thunderclouds and open sky. She hustles off, creaky-wheeled, my coffee forgotten.

A smoke it is then.

The cramped airplane bathroom is little better than a pit toilet. I guzzle my chemo pills with tepid water from a soggy Dixie cup and the plane shakes and I get baptized—gray-blond five o'clock shadow glittering with water drops, my reflection gleaming dimly in the milky cataract of a mirror. Mine is a good face with some sleep hung on it: a face four wives have loved, five if I count my ex Mambe twice. As a kid, my daughter, Chelsea, had loved to crawl on my lap at night to kiss this face. My old man spat in it once, breath marinated in sour mash, bitter because I went AWOL from the family business of soldiering— chose law school over the leatherneck ways of the Corps. Chose conduct unbecoming, in his mind. Of a mind myself to bend the rules instead of hop to them.

I look at the obligatory No Smoking in Lavatory sign below the mirror and the detector I disabled just above.

I take a long drag.

I huff. I puff.

Smells like menthol and shit in here. Someone didn't flush.

I flush. Better.

Back in my seat, I pick up coffee-grounded country reports—half their stats fabricated by me. Christ. I'd done my job too well. Only two decades removed from the first Z outbreak and now African zombies, initially a cause célèbre, were the celebrity cause du jour. Championed by aging rockers and silver fox actors with Cheshire grins. There were star-studded telethons held to raise funds for their rehabilitation into society. Every Hollywood A-lister wanted to accessorize with an African zombie baby of their very own. Those "undead" tots were trainable! Early vaccination worked!

But the photos in my folio tell a different story. No glamour shots there, just what remained of a formerly photogenic film siren, recognizable only by the longitude and latitude tattoos on her mangled shoulder blade. Her latest adopted child—one Anasta Mbengwi, age four, zombie—had made a happy meal of her. Her bottle-blond nemesis's fan base on "Team J" would be ecstatic, if I ever let them find out about this.

• • •

Back to Orliac and the big reveal. I was looking through a glass pane thick as Einstein's eyeglasses. On its flip side, Test Subject 13, nicknamed Lazarus.

Lazarus looked nothing like the late-night TV creations: shambolic shufflers, gray-fleshed and caterwauling like amateur sopranos. His skin was part nacreous, part necrotic—covered in sores I later learned came from radiation exposure. Sure, he was walking and talking like you and me and other beasts of our kind. But he was undead. Sure, he was only a bit slower, pausing every now and then to tune to some frequency beyond our ken. He was still undead. Sure, he was nothing like the creature that would sink canines and incisors into my flesh six months later. Yet he was still undead, undeader, undeadest.

Too big for my britches, my father would say, just young, dumb, and full of cum. I was twenty-nine years old and dumbstruck, gawping like some slack-jawed yokel. Maybe I was greener than I cared to admit. Maybe the fear for my wife and kid at home, in the dark, had me shook. Maybe it was normal to feel unsteady in a world gone all Tilt-A-Whirl off its axis. Or maybe it was the eerie lab full of doctors unabashedly pawing at nature and her tender parts. All these things come to mind but at the time I told myself that it was the job, just the job. Lazarus being the worst type of PR nightmare—the headlining kind: *African Super Virus Kills, Regenerates Dozens!*

Africa was on the brink, poised to become Typhoid Mary for the pandemic of the century. It seemed inevitable, this Dark Continent long plagued by germophobes nattering that her darkness was somehow catching. The first colonial conscripts who braved her shores had been petrified. Clutched their pith helmets in death grips along with trusty pamphlets on overcoming her dangers: bloodthirsty natives (Exterminate all the Brutes!), dusky nubiles threatening moral turpitude, and for those yet to fall to that particular brand of bodily corruption, there were untold diseases. Always disease. Malaria. Yellow fever. Cholera. AIDS had an entire continent scapegoated, accused of bedding down with primates. (Fast-forward a few decades and it's all: Howdy, Ebola. Welcome to the hoedown. The Canadians are mixing up a special drug cocktail just for you. But let's just keep that on international ice, tucked in some fridge till us good white folks start dying, for a sip.) That's what I was up against.

Orliac was making noises at me then, gestures too. His yapping coalesced into things called "findings." It seemed, besides the considerable trick of undying, Lazarus there wasn't getting any older. They were still running preliminary tests but five weeks of observation and the man hadn't aged a lick. That I could spin: *African Super Virus the Secret of Eternal Life!* But no. I was to keep things hush-hush and under wraps while they conducted further research. My job: quash media tales of undead relatives making any surprise *Guess Who's Coming to Dinner?* appearances. Easy enough in those halcyon days, before the internet and citizen journalists, blogs and vlogs, Tumblr and Instagram, Facebook and Twitter, YouTube and Snapchat, and so on and so on. The city folk—readers of the *Cameroon Tribune, Jeune Afrique,* and *Le Monde*—were civilized. Mean understanding of things left to their backwoods relatives with ridiculous notions of uncles and aunties and wives and daughters and mothers and fathers freshly returned to them from death's uncanny valley, tags and receipts intact.

Lazarus lulled us into complacency, that one. Orliac's team had accounted for twelve hundred of the affected, treated and studied in secret. We thought we had it all under control. Nixed the bloodshed. The violence.

It wasn't till six months later, when a gendarme pulled one named Naaman out of a dusty Kondengui prison cell for show-and-tell, that I began to truly understand the weight and heft of what I was up against. Because that thing—so docile, nearly bovine in its cud-chewing tranquility—snarled once, lunged forth, and bit me.

That long-ago night, after that thing took teeth to the meat of my hand, I hadn't really felt anything for a moment, just the shock of finding myself rent from reality, thrust into the starring role of some direct-to-video, B-movie reel. Then the gendarme took a machete in hand—those banana republic cops always seemed to have one at the ready—and cut mine clean off. Then, fuck me, it hit hard: a world of primal hurt and doomsday visions and mortal wounds came screaming down like a pack of howler monkeys, shaking the root of me till all my limbs but the one now gone were quaking. Another man might have doubled over in pain. This man heard *his* old man: *Quit your belly-aching, dogface!* So I braced myself against the shock—gnashing up the soft lick of my lip, spitting blood, steadied on a smelling salt whiff of my own briny sweat. I remember picking up my sorry hand then, cradling the suckling babe of it to my chest, before a rush of others gushed in, grabbed hold of me, and then I was away. Last thing I saw of that cell was the gendarme, in a corner, hacking that creature to bits with a brute efficiency that spoke of long practice, the deadly precision of thwacks and thwacks and thwacks on end.

● ● ●

An hour after my plane finally slouches into Douala, I'm at the orphanage founded by our recently deceased starlet after her stint as UN ambassador on mission to the Z refugee camp where she plucked her daughter. I'm being thoroughly briefed by child psychologists, preeminent Z scientists—Orliac disciples—who assure me that the thing that my photos are declaring is not possible. The children do not attack. They are not even zombies, just legally classified as such for government and international aid to the descendants of the original Nyos victims.

Finally, I am taken by a Swiss nun to meet Anasta, poster child for Z adoption.

"She's still a bit shaken, understandably," says the nun. "Sweet child. Mercifully, she can't remember a thing."

"And the father?"

"Here by tomorrow. En route from a film set somewhere. Prague, I think."

"Do you think she did it, Sister?"

"I pray not. But mine is not to judge God's ways nor his creatures," she says, unclasping the steeple of her hands to wave at a door. "Here we are."

I nod and show my ID and clearance docs to the gendarme stationed just outside. He's a lumbering hulk of a man, more matter than mind, with an AK-47 slung casually across the barrel of his bandoliered chest. He eyes my glossy laminate credentials with more than a little bit of suspicion, looking over at the sister—*Agnes, was it? Or Mary Margaret?*—for assurances that all is on the up and up. She nods, nearly imperceptibly. The fingers on my gun hand twitch, itching for the trigger of the hog's leg shooter I'd surrendered at the security desk up front. Right about now, with two hours of sleep in the last twenty-four hours, I'm doing my level best to keep from wringing this peabrain's neck and marching through this goddamn door.

Finally, he hands back my lanyard and waves me into a dayroom too sunny for such ghoulish business. Inside, Anasta is playing with her dolly. When she looks up at me, I see she is lovely in the strange way these children of Nyos can be: frosted plum skin, silver halos around her irises, as if she is being influenced by better angels.

"Hello, Anasta, I'm Connor. May I sit?"

She smiles shyly. And just like that, I'm back to my best "teatime with Chelsea" behavior as I settle into a sunflower-patterned chair, too small by far.

"Do you know what's going on?" I ask.

"Yes. New Mommy is dead. I'm not," she says. "I never was."

She's one of those tweeners, born of a mother who had been exposed to the gas but died much, much later. She looks at me. Unblinking.

The psychologists say it's hard to get a read on these kids. Something about the eyes, the affect.

"You're not real," she says, placing her dolly's hand over my prosthetic one. Brown plastic palming beige.

"Sometimes, I can be," I say.

"You smell too." She crinkles her nose, then sniffs for good measure. "But it's nice. Like Old Mommy—like honey and dirt. New Mommy and I visited her in the ground last week. She sleeps there now."

Grave beds are comfy that way.

I had prepaid for a full funeral package when I learned about my cancer a year ago. Inoperable. No joy. A five-year prognosis tops. Plenty of time to plot my escape from this illness and her harpy's grip. Pretty sure somewhere, despite the research restrictions, Orliac and his cronies are in some subterranean lab, cooking up my salvation. So there's that.

• • •

Dead man walking. Didn't know it all those years ago, but Lazarus had kin in the country, kissing cousins among the Bakweri tribe of north Cameroon. They were called the *vekongi*—victims snared by *nyongo* witchcraft, doomed to a half life: withered existence by day and entranced enslavement on the farmlands of their "masters" by night. Their distraught families had recourses of course: they could consult a witch doctor who practiced "good medsin" or an attorney who practiced criminal law. The first might involve a retainer—say a jug of palm wine, two or three goats, and a minor cash outlay; the second required a much larger sum of CFA francs, beyond the means of many of those simple village folk, but if you could afford it, justice in the courts could be yours under section 251 of the Cameroonian Penal Code for the prosecution of witchcraft practitioners. Another remedy? Mob justice—villagers stoned suspected witches and sorcerers.

Learned all this from Mambe. She was Bakweri. She was also the mother of my only child, Chelsea. When Chelse' was little, she loved bedtime stories. Anything with wicked witches and goblins and ornery ogres collecting tolls to cross rickety wooden bridges. Fancied all things monstrous. Scarier the better. Put her right to sleep.

"Once upon a time," I'd start, "there was a handsome vampire—"

"Vampires are for wussies, Dad."

"Got it. There was a handsome prince who had three wives—"

"*Kongi* wives?"

Kongi was her shorthand for the *vekongi*—for imaginary revenant relatives.

"Wait for it," I said, then continued. "One by one his three wives mysteriously died, yet the prince's lands grew fertile and his kingdom flourished. Strange fruits hung low from his trees. Crops as tall as buildings sprang up from his fields. The villagers rejoiced and filled their bellies till their guts clenched with fullness. No living soul worked his farm but by cock's crow his fields were ploughed through and through."

"*Kongi* farmers?"

"Wait for it . . ."

We went through this a thousand and one nights. My noggin chockful of a hundred ways to scare my little girl shitless, but she always, always laughed it off. Worked herself up into a drowsy stupor. I came to think of those story times as my daughter's dress rehearsal for facing life's terrors head-on. She learned to embrace the monsters under her bed, to cuddle them close as a teddy.

Her mother hated the whole thing of course, but was I really going to listen to a woman who named our daughter after a British football team? Could have been worse, I guess. Could have been Manchester. Said as much to Mambe once. Then ducked immediately. She had a good throwing arm, that one—a grinding stone (missed me), books (took an unabridged dictionary in the hip), a cell phone (head-on), slicing a scar on my left temple shaped like a reaper's sickle. An omen of things to come? Damn, I don't know. I'd lived on the continent too long, gone native, started to see signs and portents in dust tracks, in moonbeams.

• • •

"Hungry," I hear Anasta say, her voice cotton candy and light, even as I flash to an image of her tiny pearly whites marbled red with blood. Flash to Naaman's teeth clamping down on my own mitt. I suppress a shudder.

"Did you get hungry, sweetheart? Is that what happened?"

"Hungry?" she says, offering me a tea-plated sugar cookie.

I accept Anasta's hospitality and eat the cookie.

Acceptance.

Kübler-Ross should give me a medal. After my diagnosis, I'd made it through her five stages of grief—denial (a river in Africa, Chelse' would have joked, as much a fan of knock-knock and other cheesy jokes as her mother), anger, bargaining, depression, acceptance—in one month flat. 'Course I fought it. Let them cut and gut and irradiate me. Let some guru give me shark fin enemas to tack a few more years on this grizzled life of mine. Somehow, I mustered. I cared. Who knew impending death would be so life affirming? Coughing up blood tends to make a man sort certain things out.

Anasta is eating her cookie in contained little bites. Tears are falling down her cheeks but not a sound escapes past that sugary morsel.

"Hey, kiddo. What's a matter?"

She shakes her head. Comes over to me then. Scampers up onto my lap for a hug, small face upturned, looking me dead in the eye. A moment, maybe two, later, says, "My mommies are together now."

And there is something in the steadiness of her gaze, in the curve of her jaw that reminds me of my daughter, of how she could look her fears straight in the eye and not be diminished.

And before I know it, I'm hugging her back.

Acceptance.

I've had my papers in order: the bulk of things to Chelsea, waiting on her; something for each of the wives, despite the fact I still haven't told any of them, even the ones still speaking to me. If I could have put it in a press release, or 27-9-3'ed it, I'd have been golden. Delivering other people's bad news, that was what I was good at. This past year, I've been working pro bono for a couple of Morts-Vivants education programs. Named an endowed scholarship to one after my daughter. Hope she'll run it one day even after I'm long gone. I like to think she would be the kind of woman who would embrace these creatures, see them as plenty more than monsters. I like to think she would be proud that I do the same.

• • •

Saved me way back then, Mambe did. Hallucinating her for days. Conjure woman that she was. I was in isolation for a week after that thing bit me. His name was Naaman, or at least that was what the scientists called the remains they tested, Test Subject 1202. Even if his family could have been reached or notified, hardly anything remained of his immortal soul or his mortal body to identify him as anyone or anything meant to be loved or reckoned with.

Orliac and his team had commandeered a floor on the west wing of the Cameroonian president's private clinic to treat the influx of ministers and other government muckety-mucks who demanded some kind of vaccine. Unthinkable that they should somehow suffer with the masses. *Pussies.* Till this day I still suspect Z-Destruct was a syringe full of sugar water and vitamin C, but they were falling all over themselves for a shot in the ass.

So there I was. Bedbound but high-flying on a morphine wire. Caspers, more foul than friendly, floated in: poking, prodding. She: all that tethered me in that twilight limbo twixt the quick and the dead. Mambe. Mambe. Mambe, in the beginning, in the Eden before—the doubts, the recriminations, the second divorce. Mambe, an itsy-bitsy thing, in the teeny-weeniest of polka dot bikinis, lying alongside me on a Kribi beach, full of vim and vigor and secrets well kept. Head flung back to the selfsame sun that was boring through the sizzling skin dead center of my eyes, striking at the rich, bubbling oil of my desires. I want. Her to want me. To want.

"My poor *mukara*," she had cooed. *Mukara. Gai-jin. Gwai-lo. Gringo. Oyibo.* Outsider. White man. Barely into my twenties but I'd already heard them all; a drill sergeant's son who'd spent half my life under foreign suns on every base known to man. A different burning crept under my skin. Damn this woman and her sawing, parting up all that God and country and reveille-hour drills from age ten on had wrought. She would undo me. Best turn tail, I thought, but she was having none of that. Straddled me lickety-split. My hot cheeks cupped in the slick of her sun balmy hands.

"My poor, poor *mukara*," she said, eyes flashing with laughter.

I pulled her closer. Eyes closed. Her forehead to mine. Her inhale my exhale.

"Why are you crying?" she whispered. Fingers pressed to my skin, to my manic pulse.

Was I? Guess so. Thought the drip was sweat. Wasn't ready to talk about it though. I was raw, fresh from the Sudan in the bad ol' days, years in a Khartoum embassy Marine detachment, then more on a private security detail. I was good and tired. To the marrow tired. That day with her too perfect for talk of boy soldiers with guns taller than their bodies entire; pissing their pants as death took them; crying for long gone mothers in Dinka, in Nuer. Wasn't ready to talk so I kissed her to reach oblivion. And when I finally pulled away, she pulled me back. As hot and full of need as I ever could want.

"You look like crap," a voice said. Jolting me awake in the hospital bed. I jerked upright. Could've keeled over, been floor paint, but I was anchored by tubes tapping my veins. Was I still hallucinating?

Mambe was right there. Bedside. And seeing her sobered me right up. Owed her my life in more ways than one. Her father was a high-ranking minister—one of only a handful of men in the country who could A-okay VIP care for a chump like me.

"Scratch that. You look like the crap that shit poops out," she said.

"Always a pleasure to see you." I made a mock courtly gesture with the one hand left to me. Then pressed its nails into the last scar she'd given me, trying to scratch an itch just under my skull. It always acted up when she was around.

She laughed. Reached out for my missing right hand reflexively, shuddered, then reached out again to pull my bandaged stump into the cradle of her palms.

"It's good to see you too, Con," she said. She called me Con—short for my last name, Connor. Long on innuendo.

"Yes, Maim." Short for Mambe. Long on innuendo.

"Ouch," she said, holding up my stump. "For once, I had nothing to do with your stitches." She laughed, then asked quietly, "You okay? What happened? They won't tell me anything."

I shrugged. I had been foggy on the particulars myself, so doped up the first few days that Orliac's antiseptic explanations poured into ears full of cotton wool.

"Too much *Dawn of the Dead* hysteria," I said finally.

Turns out my hand was missing because some numbnut prison guard watched too much late-night television, called himself trying to "staunch the contagion," keep it from stir-frying my brain pan. Orliac had since discerned that the condition didn't work that way.

"There's nothing to be afraid of. It's not airborne, blood-borne. You either got it at Nyos or you didn't." I said this bit with a lot more conviction than I actually felt. Who was I really trying to convince? Her? Or me?

"For fuck's sake! Don't handle me, Con. Is that the truth or are you 'on message'? You've known about these mon . . . these things, for six months. You never said a word. You have a child, you have m . . ."

She looked at me piercingly. Her nails dug into my stump. I winced.

What could I say or do to make it right? Apologize? Grovel? Quote some official statement chockful of my own ten-dollar-worded BS on *homeland security reporting stratagems*? No. She deserved better. Thought about my daughter then. Her trusting beddy-bye hugs for a father who swore he'd keep her safe from night terrors and whatever else life had in store. I answered her as honestly as I could manage. "It's what they tell me, darlin'. But if you get a chance, I think you and Chelse' should take a vacation somewhere nice. Hospitable."

"Thank you, Connor." She looked me dead in the eye for a heartbeat, then peered off into some distance I knew I would never reach again. She left me then. My better half.

Last I ever saw of her. Never saw Chelse' again either—she'd be about 29/30 now. Looked for years after I stepped out of that hospital bed and into the fray. After I got back to playing my role as a cog in the world's vast meaning-making machine. My own meaning lost.

• • •

A voice is chirping, "Daddy! Daddy!"

Chelsea? I shake my head, exorcise my ghosts quick-like, hoary-headed bastard that I am.

"Daddy! My daddy's here!" It's Anasta, up and bouncing cheerily toward a violently pulsing door I'd had the good sense to lock behind me. Someone's pounding away. *The fuck?*

I'm up out of my seat bounding toward her, a teeny chair armrest strung around my left ankle. I punt it toward a corner and just as I reach the door—swooping up Anasta, dolly and all—it splinters open. Here's Sister Agnes/Mary Margaret, or some such, panting and pink-faced, the muscleman in camos in tow.

"They know," she says on a gasp, hand at her throat. "They know about the child."

And just then I hear the distinct *rat-a-tat-tat* of gunfire at the compound's gates. Peering through the dayroom's blinds, I see smoke from afar. One, maybe two, klicks south of the main building. The orphanage, ironically situated on the sprawling grounds of a defunct game reserve, had land to spare. That distance would buy us time.

Camo boy is at the door, hanging off its hinges now, radioing someone—*anyone!*—for assistance. I'd seen what passed for security around these parts so I wasn't holding my breath. The Born-Agains militia, zombie poachers—out here in the sticks we're pretty much sitting ducks for any yahoo with a grudge and a gun. More shots fired.

Closer now. Ear-shattering. What are these guys packing? What are they even shooting at? Wasted bullets riddling the clouds. Confetti ammo in the air.

Time to pop smoke!

"Sister, we need to haul ass out of here," I say. Plotting a route to my gun.

Anasta is trying to wiggle free from my arms, saying, "Movie, movie. Daddy's movie. *Pow, pow, pow.*" She shoots off tiny finger pistols.

My mind shoots to the actor's last action flick, *Resurrection Hill*—a critical flop that was box office gold. Anasta must have been on set.

"Just like Daddy's movie, sweetheart," I tell her. "You're gonna do everything me and the reverend mother say so the bad guys don't get us, right?"

She nods yes, then stills in my arms. Goes quiet as the grave.

I hand her over to the nun and we head out. Footfalls echoing in the empty hallways. Most personnel still at the older facility in the capital: the one protesters camp outside of, spewing spray-painted hate along its walls. This was supposed to be a sanctuary—isolated, safe. The best-laid plans. The security desk up front is empty, a swivel chair overturned on the floor. My holster there, my gun gone. The soldier and I exchange a look. Without a word he passes me a peacemaker, the Walther PPK from his ankle holster. The sister opens up a reception desk drawer, drops in her rosary, and pulls out a bowie knife big as my forearm. *Well I'll be damned, Mother Superior.*

She catches my look.

"Brazzaville." All she says before leading us away, down, down, down another passage. Me bringing up the rear. Watching our six as we run from the thump of gun blasts grown louder and nearer. We stop short at a steel door, more fortified than the other, this one with codes, with touchscreen panels, all manner of high-tech gizmos and sci-fi doohickeys alien to this land.

"I was stationed there for the First and Second Congo Wars," says the nun, leaning into a panel and the door slides open smooth as butter, her smile rueful as she explains the rest: "The archdiocese sent me here for peace and quiet in my final years. Then came Naaman."

. . .

Why did Naaman and others like him start to turn? Damned if I know. By the end, maybe a quarter of them would go that way. They would be calm for an eternity, the meek inheriting the earth, then something would just snap, render them id and leathery instinct and gnawing anger. No one knew why. I had a theory I never shared with Orliac. Refined on nights when I was sauced and given to panty-waist philosophizing. I thought about times when the living was easy, about dying hard—collapsing in the midst of a dead run from your hut, fleeing for your life, hard-scrabble though it was, then it's all over, all that existence and subsistence. But then it's not, there's a second chance, but you are different now, naught but a sleepwalking version of yourself, the you of you yowling—"wake up, wake up"—inside. Then one day you do.

You know the rest. There were many killings, other Namaans who took life, not just limb. Then came calls for answers, followed by government crackdowns and goose-stepping suppression. Next thing we knew, Nyos families started fleeing with the afflicted, crossing borders into tent camps. Some surlier host governments took drastic measures. Borders were closed, emergency Organization of African Unity meetings held. Orliac was subpoenaed, gave testimony at the UN as death squads drove zombie population numbers so low that there were only about three hundred confirmed cases a decade ago. Amnesty International launched "Z Rights Are Human Rights" campaigns to keep them safe from whack jobs both domestic—certain indigenous parties believed gorging on Z parts granted life eternal—and abroad—like the Born-Agains, a militant religious group that violently spread their "God Hates Zombs" message by any means necessary. But at just three hundred worldwide, the Nyos survivors were containable, nonthreatening. A source of pity in the West—with calls to designate them as an endangered "species" and keep them on a reservation—but still stigmatized in their homeland, even after the Cameroonian government created the ill-funded Departement des Affaires des Morts-Vivants.

My job once the truth was out: press conferences, informational films and billboards for the public; behind the scenes at negotiations with power brokers (sure, Big Agro can sell Africa grossly subsidized cotton and GMO corn at twice the price of our local markets, just keep those aid packages coming). You have to understand that people wanted to be lied to; they put their trusting hands in mine to willingly traipse down that garden path. They didn't really want to stare into that abyss, to reckon with its crags and ice and deep-burning fires. A lot of Africans were different, though; they lived by the pit, gazed into its bottom plenty, haggled and bargained with dwellers therein for that new government job or enough school fees for that whip-smart tenth child of theirs and, if they were lucky, just a bit of that sugarcane to make their bitter lives sweeter. These folks have touched the slithery underbelly of darkness, so they never quite bought the snake oils I was selling, but that's all right, my particular bill of goods was meant for others—for antsy international investors, for crusading human rights activists, for the US State Department.

Yes, some who died early on in the hot zones might have been saved had my spin-doctoring been less convincing. But then there's that which was saved: minds kept from shattering, economies kept from collapsing. Remember when that swine flu flare-up practically kneecapped the British economy? Can you even imagine what would have happened to those teeter-tottering African GDPs if the truth had gotten out? Talk about a shit storm, financial FUBAR.

Look, I'm fine with what I did. Sleep like a baby. Like Chelsea. In my condition, I've come to terms with many a thing. I'm sure this might make me a monster to some. But I've met real monsters and trust me, I don't come close.

• • •

"*Arretez-vous! Arretez!*" a voice yells from behind as a bullet comes shrieking past my head. I'm halfway through the steel door but I instinctively pivot to a knee and fire. Two bodies thud to the ground. For a split second, I'm twenty years old, a pissant grunt in Sudan again, then—*pop!*—another shot snaps me back, has me up and running through the steel door, straight into a panic room—those tailor-made bunkers beloved by Hollywood pooh-bahs and Saudi sheikhs flush with petrodollars and paranoia. Barely got my left foot in before the door clangs shut behind me. Soldier boy, manning the control panel, shrugs at my scowl, tipping his head toward the CCTV screens showcasing jackbooted thugs, in grime-spattered wife beaters and ratty cargo pants, ripping through the hallways. Armed up the wazoo. Shooting indiscriminately at lamps and computer screens alike. *Jesus.*

The control panel says we're locked in tight. I turn in search of the sister, finding her in a smaller room, kneeling next to a pallet by the wall. There is blood everywhere. But no one is screaming.

"Sister?"

"Not me." She moves slightly and I see Anasta's slight form on the makeshift bed. "It's the girl. She's been s-h-o-t."

Like spelling it out will hide the truth from the child. There is a seeping bullet wound on a thigh that looks too tiny to make a worthy target. It's bleeding all the same. My one step forward has me swaying like a willow. I check to see if I'm shot too.

No.

Step one. *Steady.* Two. *Steady.* Steadier still as I reach the bed and drop to my knees on the floor beside her. Anasta's eyes are closed. She looks peaceful.

"She will live," the sister says, patting my hand. "It's barely a flesh wound and the young heal so much faster than we. Praise God."

"She'll live," I say out loud, testing the weight of it in the air.

I let out a breath I hadn't realized I'd been holding. Let loose a ragged chuckle. *Dumbass.* Here's me roiling with fear, panties twisted, worried that a dead girl might die.

She'll live. Because I am dead too, you see. So what I've been walking and talking and fighting and fucking just like any other creature that God whispered life into. The deep, deep spark of me was snuffed out the moment I lost Mambe and Chelsea. Just didn't know it for a while, not till I sat in an office looking at another doctor in a lab coat tell me what I already should have known. I was a dead man walking.

But I'll live. After a sort.

Three hours later there are 'copters. Then sirens. Then the rescue. That ragtag team of would-be insurgents long gone. Toting everything in the joint that wasn't nailed down.

Three days later, we will learn that the Born-Agains mounted the siege. Eventually, even this country's forensics will catch up to my investigation and we'll discover that the star's death was staged by that selfsame group, attacking her and her child "abomination," siccing dogs on the screen idol to drum up anger around an alleged zombie attack. But that version of events is too inflammatory, the government will say. Bad press. So the perpetrators will be punished quietly. Locked away in some dank cells much like the hoosegow I visited all those years ago. And I will craft my patented "princess" cover story—"Death by Automotive Misadventure." Plausible enough given Cameroon's notoriously treacherous roadways.

This is what we will tell the fair-haired father when he swoops in, cameras flashing, to collect his convalescing child. This is what we will tell you. The only truth you'll ever know. And you'll accept it because you once set out sugar cookies for Santa, you trust deeply in the power of your voice and your vote, and expect that when you die, when you are nothing but bone and bliss, there lies a new beginning, a sweet hereafter.

The Statistician's Wife

Statistics are human beings with the tears wiped off.
—PAUL BRODEUR

They were bloodhounds worrying a bone. The two homicide detectives sniffed, smelled something off in the pairing of this forty-year-old Boston Brahmin and his young village bride. Elliot Coffin Jr. was as American as Coca-Cola, and capitalism. The bland portfolio of his upbringing was made of *Happy Days* and hedge funds in happier days, pre-Madoff. He was undisputedly American. His recently deceased wife—Victoria Coffin, née Chiamaka Victoria Okereke, recently of Cambridge, Massachusetts, by way of Lagos State, Nigeria—was not. These simple facts, on their surface, so nakedly banal in nature, had kept Coffin Jr. moored in the sterile Cambridge PD interrogation room, even as his wife lay below on a steel slab in the morgue, soul hovering, body beginning the slow decay that would solidify the truth of her death.

The detectives observed him through a one-way looking glass. The man before them had slate-gray eyes, seemingly void of grief, set deep in a handsome, angular face of severe symmetry broken only by a nose whose slight crook hinted that he could take a punch, or perhaps deliver one. The very definition of buttoned up: this man in navy-blue Brooks Brothers and Presidential pocket square, in a custom-fit Turnbull & Asser of crisp, creaseless white. Too quiet, he was, as if the intricate Eldredge knot of his silk tie were a garrote at his throat. Too sharp, he was, the obstinate geometry of his frame leaving you with the overall impression that if you brushed against him, however slightly, you might bleed.

He put the detectives on edge.

Coffin Jr. was an economist—no, statistician, he'd insisted—from a well-respected family: a financier father, a bepearled mother. But the girl in the morgue, just a girl, hardly a wife, was no blueblood. In the couple's wedding portrait, now bagged and blood-splattered in evidence, she was soft and cocoa-skinned, like the sweet promise of uncut brownies.

———

Data Set Entry: August 10, 2005. Euless—Dallas suburb. Johnny Omorogieva, 45, from Edo State, murdered his RN wife, Isatu Omorogieva, 35, also from Edo State, repeatedly striking her on the head with a hammer in front of their 7-year-old daughter.

———

"Why don't you start from the beginning, Mr. Coffin?" asked the detectives in tandem, a Greek chorus of interrogation. "Where were you this morning?" Their questions anchored him. For some time now Elliot's thoughts had been fluid, even as a slice of his consciousness remained alert. He had always had a particularly tidy mind: compartmentalized, cubicles of awareness, now calculating and assessing his surroundings, his circumstances. He noted the taller detective, barely inching past his partner, had passed a hand through his rusty-nail head of hair ten times, waiting. He noted the second hand on the bulbous wall clock was off by 2.5 seconds, exactly. He time-lined the tragic particulars of his morning: relaying the data to them as neutrally as he could, maintaining a barely managed remove, even as a part of him silently screamed his innocence, while another grieved.

"I wake up at five on the dot every day," said Elliot, breathing in deeply to steady himself, remembering the heady aroma of Ethiopian Sidamo coffee from that morning. "I noticed that Vicky's side of the bed was empty but nothing felt amiss. Not yet."

On Thursday mornings, he told them, his RN wife worked the eleven-to-seven shift at St. Joseph's Nursing Home and Assisted Living the night before. This morning he woke up. He rose. Shuffled barefoot to the kitchen—Vicky has, *no, "had," remember*, had a habit of borrowing his slippers and shedding them anywhere and everywhere but bedside. He had moved through the TV-less TV room, then through the dining room, his footsteps keeping time with the *tick-tock* of an octogenarian grandfather clock, a family heirloom, ostensibly a wedding gift from his parents, but really, only his mother. In the kitchen he'd fixed a cup of already percolating, preset joe. The fair-trade kind Vicky insisted upon. He'd yet to turn on a single light, had no need to, in fact, the predawn hallways imprinted on him, despite having lived there merely a few short months.

Their Beacon Hill home was his wedding present for a wife whose body lay cooling in a small pool of blood at the far end of the kitchen island even as he went outside for the morning paper. He had yet to find her. No, not yet. He'd read the paper. Had his morning constitutional. It was after. Only after retracing his steps—*tick-tock, tick-tock*—after the need for a second cup drew him to his private reserve of *kopi luwak*, hidden deep in the recesses of a cupboard's topmost shelf, far from the disapproving harrumphs of a wife who'd deemed the harvesting of his "cat shit" coffee so unspeakably creepy and cruel she'd shamed him into a secret stash, sipped only when she was— where exactly?—he wondered, confused and foot-dragging now, bare soles gathering dust as he considered callouts and impromptu double shifts and who-the-hell-is-she-withs till he stumbled, practically tripping over her.

Before the crippling disbelief. Before the confusion/fear/rage rendered him a dark, howling thing, he had been smiling, chuckling inwardly, at the sight of one of his slippers, the right one, flung carelessly by a trash bin. *Vintage Vicky.* Stooping to retrieve it, it was then, in that moment, that he saw its mate, right there, lynched on the left foot of her prone body: her outstretched limbs in angles unnatural, knife embedded in her back to the hilt of its pearlized handle, a piece of another wedding gift, a full set, part of him dimly noted, even as another part had him screaming her name. Over and over and over again.

Everything rushed forward after that, with a relentless, almost mechanized momentum: try to revive her, try again, shake her, shout out for her, shake her, shout, call authorities, answer door, answer questions, sit in ambulance, answer questions, submit to checkup, answer questions, watch them take her, answer questions, sit in waiting room, ask them questions, sit at this table, answer questions, answer questions, answer questions. All the while, *what was your question?*, hands spasmodic—open now, now shut—as he clutches a pinstriped blue slipper—now open, shut now—stained crimson with blood and a single tangerine drop of her favorite nail polish, Siren #440.

—

Data Set Entry: January 1, 2007. Burtonsville, Maryland. Kelechi Charles Emeruwa, 41, from Old Umuahia, Abia State, was charged with, and convicted of first-degree murder after stabbing his estranged wife, 36-year-old RN and mother of three young children, Chidiebere Omenihu Ochulo.

—

"Tell us about your marriage, Mr. Coffin," the detectives prodded genially. "How long you two together? How'd you meet?"

"We were happy. Had our ups and downs, I suppose," Elliot replied, what else could he say? In couples therapy, he'd called married life "nonmonotonic," like a line graph that swings up and down, full of vicissitudes, variables aplenty. Dr. Klein misheard his one-word assessment and erroneously repeated "nonmonogamous" and Vicky, daughter of the second of ten wives herself, lost it. Together, they lost a whole session to that mishap, yet the word still struck him as astute. The ups: she has, *no, had*, dimpled cheeks and dimpled knees. A way of peeling an orange that was pure art. One fluid curl springing zestfully off her knife's edge. The downs that curved up: when they first met in Lagos, he'd been sick, she'd fed him vitamin-C-laden oranges and tangerines and clementines along with mouthfuls upon mouthfuls of *mmiri an ji*—the Igbo answer to chicken soup. He'd been bedridden, and mortified, at the time. He worked with the World Bank, for Christ's sake, was more than well traveled across a continent rife with illnesses long since conquered in other climes (he half expected bubonic plague to make a comeback there).

He was conditioned to keep his guard up. He'd taken all the requisite precautions. The regimen of shots—yellow fever, typhoid, cholera—and oral prophylactics, a grab bag of chloroquine, iodine tabs, plus the occasional herbal remedy.

It was chicanery that got him.

"You bought water from vendors on the street?" his future wife asked, barely concealing a grin.

"I was hot," he'd answered, "and it was Perrier." He grimaced at the acrid memory of its aftertaste. "So I thought."

"Perrier isn't spelled with four *r*'s."

"I repeat. I. Was. Hot." He was still hot—had a fever, in fact—and was unamused, in no mood really to be mocked by this nineteen-year-old housegirl—this Lagos parvenu from some backwater town in Anambra State. He vowed to tell his driver, Chibuzo, that this ridiculous young cousin of his just would not do, that he'd no need of a nursemaid, he was fine, really, just fine on his own. He'd weakly thrown off the thin bedsheet, which weighed down on him with the oppressive yet all-seeing heft of an X-ray bib—and her knowing stare.

"*Ndo*, you look hot," she said, faint frown clouding her brow as she put her hand to his own. Satisfied by what she felt there, she was all smiles again, handing him a bottle of water, cheekily adding, "Don't worry. *I* read the label."

For two weeks, she'd been his Nightingale, the much-ballyhooed call to Chibuzo forestalled, then put off again till he'd gotten better and gotten back to work. On the evening of his third day back at the office, he came home to find her waiting on his steps, a covered food dish place-set on an Anatomy and Physiology book, all balancing on her knees.

Without a word, he took her in.

After that, she'd come daily: to feed him, to tidy, to finish homework on his computer. She was a nursing student. She teased him relentlessly about being her toughest clinical case. He grew accustomed to her: taught her chess, the Sicilian Defense, and how to sacrifice a queen. But mainly they talked. Or rather she talked—about her classes, her fledgling coin collection—and he listened. By turns, she drew him out. While he absolutely refused to ride the *okada* motorcycles or *danfo* buses that *put-putted* across the megacity's pockmarked streets—playing chicken with pedestrians and motorists alike—he did allow Vicky to show him *her* Lagos. Places beyond the high, reinforced walls of his hermetically sealed condo complex on Victoria Island.

"Las Gidi is a city that is thick and heavy like *nni ji*. Best taken in small bites," she told him, over dinner at a *bukka* chophouse, feeding him yam-*foufou* from the spoon of her fingertips. "Tasty though, no?"

Their first time was messy, feral even. They'd been lounging on the couch after supper, watching NTA TV as Chicken Little newscasters squawked on and on about yet another Nigerian airplane falling from the sky, the third in as many months. *How irritatingly predictable*, he'd thought, just as she turned to him, tears in her eyes. It was disconcerting and, and, stirring. *Strange, altogether strange.* Something moved through him, something unbidden. Unexpected. *Unwanted?* He stiffened. Gave her shoulders a glancing *there-there-now* pat. His was not a family given to grand gestures of affection, yet somehow, in-explicably, even to himself, when she responded by moving closer to him, muscling a tear-stained cheek into his crisply tailored shirtsleeve, he took her in. Something happened in his chest then, a sawing sensa-tion only vaguely reminiscent of breathing. Heartbeat tapping a stac-cato code against his rib cage. She'd looked at him, knowingly. Her upturned face saying she'd deciphered its message. So he kissed her then. Then all was chaos: teeth at his nape, nails scratching his thighs, hands fisting her braids. *Exhilarating.*

They fell for each other. The descent quick thereafter. He came to realize, quite quickly, how a man could utterly be held in sway by the *tam-tam* rhythm of a woman's hips as she walked by. For her part, she came to love him, with a raw, singular intensity that he could never have anticipated—or purchased online. Yes, purchased, that's right. He and Vicky heard the rumors later, the whispered asides of Cambridge neighbors when he'd brought her back home to the States. She must be a mail-order bride, wooed via keystroke. She was flesh trade goods from some chauvinist, male-fantasy site like Africanbeauty.com. Afrobride.com promised a selection of "elegant and lovely ladies" in a buffet of nationalities: Nigerian, Cameroonian, Ethiopian, Ivorian. Or perhaps her provenance was a sister site? One like foreignprincesses.com, where African women vied for Western Prince Charmings with international Cinderallas: Irina from Kiev, Naviya from Pattaya, Jun Li from Kunming. One day Elliot found Vicky browsing one such site, absorbed by the profile of "Sexy Kenyan Kitten," twenty-one-year-old Nadine from Nairobi, smiling coquett-ishly over a shoulder tattoo and gushing about her willingness to "cater to my man."

"Cater to you, hmph," Victoria said, sucking her teeth and jump-ing up from the computer in disgust. "Save that for an R&B song. Igbo women are warriors, don't you dare laugh, Elliot."

He laughed, watching his diminutive wife scowl up at him, one hand poised on a cocked hip, the other sprouting a wagging finger. He turned around to hide his face. "I'm not laughing." *Why was she the only one who made him laugh?* "I swear I'm not."

"Mm-hmm. You know, Elliot, when Igbo women feel disrespected, we make war on men."

He felt her grab the back of his favorite shirt, an umber guayabera, last reminder of the uniform he'd worn daily in the tropics.

"What are you—? Vicky, this is linen. You know you're buying me a new one, right?"

He heard muffled chuckling. "See me this, fashionisto. When I met you, you had *one-one* shirt." Tiny hands scaled up his neck. "Now keep quiet while I school you." She hoisted herself fully onto his back. "I'm teaching you a history lesson. So listen up."

"I'm all ears, Teach," he replied, clamping her thighs securely around him. Wondering if poor attention would earn him the ruler. Wanting it.

Vicky began her piggybacked lecture.

"In 1929, ten thousand Igbo women started *ogu umunwanyi*, the Women's War. When men do wrong, we 'sit on you.' It's part of our tradition, how we protest."

"You climbing on me. This is protest? Vicky—"

"Shhh, I'm not done, as for climbing, well, let's say I'm improvising. I could also burn your hut, but it's a very nice hut, and I live in it, too."

As he walked them to the bedroom, she proceeded to school him about mass uprisings among Igbo women in villages across Eastern Nigeria. Women protesting in droves, as Britain's colonial taxes handicapped their fledgling enterprises, the small goods and foodstuffs market that helped sustain their families. She spoke of women mobilizing, of war paint on faces, of war songs and rallying cries ringing out, of staring down enemies—the Brits, yes, but their colonial proxies, the warrant chiefs too, and local men these women knew: brothers, friends, and sometimes husbands who could be shamed. They sang, they chanted, they brought down the system.

"And the moral of this story is?" he asked, placing her on the bed for her finale.

"Always fight, never surrender," she replied, then pulled him down to the bed and covered his body with her own.

———

Data Set Entry: March 25, 2006. Garland, Texas. Theophilus Ekoh Ojukwu, 46, from Enugwu-Agu, Ihe, in Awgu LGA, Enugu State, bludgeoned RN wife, Melvina Ojukwu, 36, from Umuanebe, also of Ihe, Awgu LGA, Enugu State, with hammer. The couple had four children, ages 4 through 9. Ojukwu was sentenced to life in prison.

———

"We just want to help you, son," said the older detective, the stout one with the third button dangled loose, spilling into a coffee stain that trickled, grew girth, over the bell jar of his belly. *McManus, was it?* "We're here for you. We're here to listen."

"You listening?" asked McManus, giving his partner a look. "Maybe we're due for a break. How 'bout some coffee, son?"

Son. It was a word unfamiliar to Elliot. To Elliot Coffin Sr., he'd been "junior" or "the boy" all his life, as in *The boy is too soft, Jillian— all that Chopin, Schubert nonsense you fill his head with. Boarding school will toughen him right up. You'll see.*

At boarding school, he had mastered precisely three things: how to curse in flawless French—*casse toi, sal espèce de salope*—the entire hard-core rap oeuvre of Niggaz Wit Attitudes, and swindling in chess. He also learned, yet never quite perfected, the outsider art of beating a boy till you maimed him, body and soul.

His own beatings had gone on for a full year by then. Dating back to his arrival at the academy as a puny freshman, drowning in his crested cardigan, fair game for a sadistic set of upperclassmen. Then the summer before tenth grade he shot up a foot, then another foot that fall. That spring, he found the ringleader, Scott Lasseter, smoking weed behind the grounds building after evening prayers. A southpaw, Elliot led with his left—a roundhouse punch that connected with bone and sinew. He felt the satisfying grind of teeth against his knuckles, and after that, a darkness embraced him, blind moments before he came to. Found himself standing, fists pulpy and throbbing, looking down at the ruins of the other boy's face—eyes collapsed, mouth excavated. A part of him immediately remorseful: his stomach rolled once, turned again, bent him over, kneecapped him till he was sure he would puke, but it passed, and soon after, something else entirely gripped him, a chokehold of fierce euphoria. He felt invincible. And painfully alive.

"Drink this, Junior." Elliot's father handed him a glass. After the fight, he'd been duly expelled. After school authorities informed his parents of "the incident," he'd been sent for. Retrieved by his father's people. Left to ponder his future on the long ride home. Returned home in disgrace, to sit there, in his father's library, and wait on his final judgment. He was burning with newfound defiance, spoiling for a fight. The last thing he'd predicted was détente.

He considered the shot of whiskey at hand. It was Glenfiddich, the good stuff, housed in a cherrywood liquor cabinet that had long stood sacrosanct in the Coffin household, spoken of in hushed tones, its spirits saved for his father's solitary communions.

Elliot gulped down the shot and felt his chest burn with a different, unholy fire.

His father stood watchful, quietly sipping his own drink, while Elliot bore up under his stare. Finally, solemnly, his father spoke. "You're a man now, son."

"Drink this, son," said McManus, handing Elliot a foam cup.

Son.

It was too late to be reborn as anyone's son. In the dim room, Elliot sipped bitter coffee, thought bitter thoughts. A cold light filtered through a high window—its crocheted grating like some iron afghan thrown over the lap of the world. He felt a chilling apprehension. He knew he was trapped. He'd run through several variables in his head. Conclusion: stay put. He needed to be here, to cooperate, to answer questions and prepare himself to face whatever trumped-up charges these detectives dared to concoct.

———

Data Set Entry: June 16, 2010. Tampa, Florida. Olufemi Ademoye, 56, charged with second-degree murder in Florida for allegedly killing his wife, Juliet Oluwatoyin Ademoye, 52, over the paternity of the couple's 17-year-old son.

———

They kept at him. What was your wife into? Any hobbies?

Did your wife have any enemies, Mr. Coffin? *No.*

Any new "special friends"? *Yes.*

Victoria was a whirligig. There were tons of new friends and new activities since the move to Cambridge. Freed from the shackles of her elder cousin's arbitrary curfews and assorted Lagos transportation constraints, she went everywhere. With everyone but him it seemed. There was pottery on Mondays with Kurt—*Nkem, darling, don't worry, he's gay*—or Saturday-morning Pilates with Karen—*You know her, Elliot, the neighbor in the house with the yellow shutters, yes, the ones you hate.* But it was never the neighborhood friends and work friends that caused the panicky, angry burn in the pit of his stomach that he slowly came to recognize as jealousy. It was her coins, or rather, their bestowers.

Back in Lagos, she'd been a collector, had a cache of currency gifted to her by the globe-trotting clients Chibuzo ferried across the sprawling city. She had coins, and only coins, since her cousin made a habit of seizing the banknotes as his so-called commission. They weren't particularly old or valuable, more aged by pocket grime than time, but it was the sentimental value she placed on them that gave him pause. There was a coppery ¥0.5 piece embossed with a lotus flower given to her by Yen—a Shanghai businessman who called her *little lotus blossom* in his frequent emails. A Sacagawea from a Texan engineer that she claimed to love because Lewis and Clark's Shoshone guide was memorialized toting a baby on her back à la Igbo. But she was cradling it in her hand one day and he swore he heard her whisper "Howdy."

"You're going away? Again?" he'd asked over dinner one night. Quiet as she'd rattled off her schedule for the upcoming weeks.

"The trip's in two weeks, Elliot. And it's only for one day, a spa day."

He fell silent. It was only a day, to be sure, only a day. One of few he could spare from work, a day better spent together, walking along the Charles or playing chess in the Square.

"*Biko*, Elliot, please. You know I didn't come all the way to America, all the way to *obodo oyibo*, to sit in the house all day." She was up then, clearing the plates, leaving him there, at the table alone, clutching a steak knife in his hand, all but forgotten, till he came to and saw blood.

He went out into a starless night. Wrapped a bandage around his blooded skin in the privacy of their wraparound porch. He knew there'd be no sleeping tonight, his mind damned to replay their dinner's fallout, dragging him through hell and back, then unto wakefulness, his palms itchy and reaching out, rooting blindly for the comfort of his sleeping wife's skin, as he'd done so many a night, now second nature, surprised to feel fingers, *his fingers*, landing, then curling slowly, around the nape of her supple neck.

The darkness embraced him.

On the porch, hands clenched, his fingers curled around the *clink-clink* clatter of metal. When had he picked up her coins? Those tokens of other men's affections. One day would he too be part of her bygone collection? Chibuzo had implied as much, told Elliot he was just an *onye ocha* meal ticket. Cursed him for never giving *kola*, paying bride price for Vicky's hand. Elliot was no fool, he knew some women on the continent used "bottom power," used the currency of their bodies to acquire jobs, status, and the all-protective power of being "Mrs. So-and-So" in a patriarchal society. But Vicky was different. She was his. *Wasn't she?*

The coins *clink-clinked* answers. Conspiring in his hand.

He wanted to hurl them.
Wanted to skip them like rocks on currents of night air.
He wanted to show his mettle.
To prove what he was worth.
So he did.

—

Data Set Entry: August 7, 2010. Exeter Township, Pennsylvania. Chukwudubem Okafor killed himself after murdering his wife, Cheryl, 37. The couple had four school-age children.

—

"We found some interesting stuff on your hard drive, Professor."

Professor. The taller detective—Murray, was it? Yes, Murray—had taken to calling him "professor." Said in the same sneering tone used for words like *Barnie* or *liberal elite*. He was an economist at a respected and renowned think tank, but as the first hour in the box segued into the fifth, frustration had worn down the veneer of politesse afforded him, worn thin the illusion that they considered him a grieving spouse and not a *person of interest*.

They slammed manila folders and reams of printouts down on the table before him. Their eyes accusatory. Their twisted lips damning. He knew what they had—his files, his raw data: the obituaries, court case briefs, blog forum transcripts, newspaper clippings (*Washington Post, Baltimore Sun, Houston Chronicle, Tampa Bay Times*)—and his own meticulous notations and graphs about uxoricide, wife killings. Nigerian wives, to be precise. His notes dispassionately appraised a couple's age, income, occupational and educational disparities to predict the probability of homicide. In the mid-aughts there had been a rash of these murders and manslaughter cases across the United States. These crimes well noted in his wife's diaspora community. Several message boards decried the lack of media coverage, more evidence of *MWWS—Missing White Woman Syndrome*. None of these murdered women had ever raised a pom-pom. None had swishy blond names like Becky or Mindy. Instead, they were nurses, with long medicinal names one had to purse one's lips to pronounce. Names as convoluted and polysyllabic as the generic drugs they dispensed at care centers, served with applesauce and Ensure.

It was Victoria who showed him the data. Of Isatu Omorogieva, Monireti Abeni Akeredolu, Melvina Ojukwu, Chidiebere Omenihu Ochulo, Uchenna Ezimora, Anthonia Iheme, all wives slaughtered, a slew of others shot, knifed, beaten, yet somehow escaping with their lives, if not their souls, intact.

"Look at this, Elliot," she said, from her perch at his desk. "These stories are crazy. These poor women. Why aren't people talking about this?"

"Not enough cases," he replied, unthinking. "Statistically negligible."

She swore at him in Igbo then, something muttered, lowing. "You have to look beyond that, Elliot. Stop crunching the numbers!"

Too late now, he understood. Only now after he had loved her and lost her. Of course, his data sets could never capture the horror of a seven-year-old daughter watching her father bludgeon her mother to death with a hammer. No histogram could model the motives that drove a man to commit such an act. He knew the stories by heart. Tales of men who had harvested brides from the village, imported them to America, offering education and elevation only to later be outgrown by That Wife. That Wife: she once was respectful, knew her place, now she fancied herself his *oga*. That Wife: she knew chapter and verse of the *oyibo* family law that *thiefed* his three children, his Lexus, his suburban duplex during the divorce. That Wife: she went to school on his *naira*, then his dollars, his three dirty jobs financed her studies. Now she had a salary and she alone clutched the purse strings. That Wife he plucked from a hovel. That Wife he handsomely paid five goats and four jugs of palm wine for. That Wife was too mouthy. That Wife had unmanned him. Madness. Elliot knew how Ekwensu's trickster spirit could worm into a man, leave a mind full of maggots. Leave you bleary-eyed and hollow with blood on your hands wondering how and why and when.

He understood these men's dark longings. Understood how a husband could want to own his wife's thoughts, own her very footsteps.

This is when she came to him. Vicky, somehow there in the box, smile seeming all too real, laughing and joking that Asasaba, ferryman to the Igbo afterlife, was running late as any *danfo* driver. Teasing him about the fine mess he'd gotten himself into, some *oyibo palava*. *O te aka o di njo, emesie o ga-adi mma.* She gave him a kiss and an orange to make it better. Then she was gone.

• • •

Elliot Coffin Jr. made his living in a field mistrusted by many. Statistics was filled with vaguely sinister terminology like *abnormal obsolescence* and *abuse of dominant position*. Working in econometrics, he dealt in numerical data and facts, the quantifiable. He knew the average price of grain in the Midwest or the number of tires sold to foreign car manufacturers. Armed with facts and figures, he had once considered himself a man of pure logic. He knew how his charts and graphs would look to a jury. So when the detectives asked him why there were no signs of forced entry, why he was the last person to see "the deceased"—he knew what they were really asking was, *Why did you kill your wife, Mr. Coffin?*

Elliot once clung to numbers, data, facts, and figures; but in this matter, they betrayed him.

———

Fact: In the United States, 33 percent of murders are intimate partner homicides—perpetrators determined to be spouses, ex-spouses, boyfriends, and girlfriends.

Fact: The percentage of intimate homicides doubles when the gender of the victim is female.

Fact: Elliot Coffin Jr. maintained that he did not kill his wife; but he would be the first to admit that, statistically speaking, he could have.

Dance the *Fiya* Dance

Tuesday, Feb. 22

Belinda is teasing me about keeping a "diary" again. And despite the lack of a gold-tone lock or the unicorn-fetish cover of my 5th grade diary, she might just be right. I've been calling this a journal but even that holdover term from my Anthro training seems too imprecise. Inside these pages are field notes, yes—page upon page of my scrawling on the phonological truncations and morphological hybridizations of broken English—yet interwoven with these entries are my personal ramblings, half-remembered recipes, sickening poems about my ex, and never-ending to-do lists. This book—diary or journal—is my mind uncensored. As much as I love my cousin, my family, my flesh and blood, theirs is a meddlesome love. In these pages I place my confidence and confidences, thoughts so private, I long for that tiny gold lock, once more.

Wednesday, Feb. 23

<u>To Do</u>—Buy milk, sugar (bake scones for Saturday—don't forget!), SlimFast, Alli, diet Coke

Reminder—Appt. at Dr. B's on Friday—the gyno question of the century: should I go off birth control? Pro: possible weight loss—a svelteness that defies my natural curviness. Con: constant reminder of singledom. Exactly whose birth am I controlling anyway?

The Baby Shower

I walk into a room of double-chinned smiles and belly laughs. Every woman—there are only women—looks ample, replete. A susurrus of sighs and coos emanates from their midst. I move closer to investigate. The source? Perpetual, the mother-to-be, happily ensconced in a ribbon-decked place of honor, a ravaged gift box balanced on the rotunda of her tummy. Strewn at her feet, gutted boxes, once fatty with BabyBjörns, day rompers, night rompers, and Diaper Genies.

"Pepe, I done reach," announces my cousin Belinda. I note the collective eye roll from the women gathered. Belinda's tardiness is legend, even in a social set where four-o'clock weddings often start at seven.

"*Chey, Belinda, you di talksay you done reach? You for come and baby done already born, oh!*" jokes one older aunty, adjusting the auburn Jheri curl wig capsized on her head.

There is a chorus of laughter. Perpetual, already cultivating an air of maternal stoicism, grants Belinda a beatific smile. Belinda bends to hug her friend, then places our present on the pile of unopened gifts under the watchful eye of Helena, who is dutifully gathering up shredded wrapping and tissue paper in frenzied colors like fuchsia! and magenta!

My stomach is growling, yet I fight the urge to nibble my store-bought scones. Instead, I place them gingerly on a table so heavily laden with food its spindly wooden legs are wobbling, knock-kneed. There is *foufou*, *ndole*, groundnut stew, *jollof* rice, plantains, *koki* corn, *koki* beans, *achu*, *gari*, and at least three kinds of chicken: stewed, roasted, and a tough bush fowl fried to the consistency of a fist.

My salad days are over.

For three weeks my simple move from New York to Washington, DC, has been complicated by wiring issues in my new apartment. I am staying with Belinda, captive to her many comings and goings. As a doyenne of the metro-area Cameroonian community, my cousin's social calendar is lousy with *cry-dies*, *born-houses*, *knock-doors*, and their pale American cousins: the funeral, baby shower, and engagement party. With so much on our plate, as it were, I feel weighed down. I need room, a space to write, research in peace, and sometimes, only sometimes, cry out at the ache that was my ex's parting gift to me a year ago. Steven had wanted me in that ribboned hot seat, but I'd balked—chosen a fellowship in Johannesburg over nappies and onesies.

On a nearby couch a platoon of women swap maternity war stories: one lifts her blush pink silk blouse to reveal a jagged C-section battle scar, another speaks of a third miscarriage followed by the triumphant delivery of six children. Tumbling out are tales of bowel movements on the labor bed, ectopic pregnancies, and attacks of preeclampsia. Calabar chalk quells prenatal nausea, but can also *enlever un bébé*, did you know? They are veterans. With stretch-mark badges of honor to prove it. I listen to them, rub my empty belly, and find I am nibbling on a scone in spite of myself. *Damn.*

"*I done reach*," says a new voice. A particularly pulpy woman strides into the room. There are no eye rolls this time. I watch her flit about, arresting, then resuscitating chatter in her wake. She is all smiles, all dimpled cheeks and dimpled arms jutting from a tight tank top bedazzled with one word: Diva. She is everywhere. She is in front of me now, or rather in front of the food table, where I hover like some wraith. I do feel somewhat uncarnate, hollowed by hunger.

"*Chop done ready?*" She rubs her stomach, eyeing the table, then me, its unofficial guardian. "*Ma belly dey bite. You no hear as it dey grumble?*"

"Well, they haven't officially opened the table." I rub my own stomach in pang-filled sympathy. "But you can have one of these."

She eyes the proffered plate of scones or perhaps my use of "grammar"—standard English—suspiciously.

"*You be na Belinda ee cousin*," then switching to English, "Chambu, right?"

"Yes, I'm Chambu, uh, Genevieve Chambu Johnson from New York—"

"The language professor?"

"Sort of, not quite. I'm a linguistic anthropologist." I hurry forward at her blank stare. "I study the relationship between languages and culture."

"Belinda said you study pidgin . . . but you don't know how to speak?"

"I do, I do. My pronunciation is just kind of slow, very *old mami*." I smirk at my own joke.

She smiles. It is not a nice smile.

I think of the gray-haired mamas I had spent my summers with in the village, mumbling our dialect and pidgin to me as they chewed kola nut—their tongues heavy with its bitter juices, with their bitter tales of feckless husbands, of jealous co-wives, of babies forfeit.

"But you grew up in Cameroon, *no be so?*"

"Yes, but I'm Halfrican. My dad is American—Brooklyn, born and raised. So he wanted us to go to the American school. No Pidgin 101 classes there. More like people asking me did I speak 'African.'" I smile.

"Hmmph, an *akata*." She says the last word with emphasis. Like my father's African American otherness explained any and all alleged shortcomings. I find myself wanting to champion my dad—a man who'd so wholeheartedly embraced his wife's homeland as his own that our village had given him the honorary title *Nwafor*.

But I don't. Instead, I turn away and find myself absently nibbling my scone again. *Damn.*

Across the room, Belinda stands in the gaggle of acolytes that always seems to spring up around her at these affairs. I feel the weight of this woman's gaze on the side of my cheek, my bare shoulder—scanning me to the bone. I turn to face her. There is a knowing half smile hooked crookedly on her lips. I've seen that look before in all its presumptuous incarnations. She's figured me out, got my number like some scratch-off lotto ticket, laid bare by a grubby coin rub. Pennies for my thoughts.

I put the scone down, my chin up. "What's your name, again?"

"Catherine Etuge—"

"Well, Cath-er-ine. I'm an *a-ka-ta*." I say the last word with emphasis, scone crumbs flying from my gesturing hand. "My two sisters and my brother are *a-ka-tas*." My voice and color are rising. "And you're living in a city full of *a-ka-tas*, making good money and a living because *a-ka-tas* died and fought for *all* Black folks' rights to—"

"Chambu. Cata. You two have met," says a cheery Belinda. Her handmaiden, the normally dour Helena, is in tow, eyes gleaming. "Chambu, Catherine is Phillip Nyami's sister."

Belinda is eyeing us both now. Me: flushed of face. Catherine: slitty-eyed, mouth agape, gulping in air like a new brand of toddler, tantrum pending.

Phillip Nyami? Ahh. That explains Helena's gleam, Belinda's cheer—a man. My cousin fancies herself a matchmaker. Under her roof, her tutelage, I will finally find a husband—correction—make that a *Cameroonian* husband, a father for my children, a man who will settle down and claim me—unlike my "useless" *akata* ex. She still doesn't know it was I who was the restless one.

I shake my head, my anger on mute.

Last night, I'd been shaking my head in refusal. I was in the car with Belinda, driving home from dropping her son off at peewee soccer practice and her daughter at ballet, when she pounced. She caught me unaware, distracted by my meditations on the radio dial, by the rare opportunity to control the music selection.

"Phillip is a good man," she began. "Don't you want children? Louchang and Meka ask me all the time, 'Mommy, when is Aunty Chambu going to have babies?' They want cousins."

Low blow, Belinda, using the twins. Low blow, indeed.

"The answer is still no, Bee," I'd said, exhaling a deep breath. "No more blind dates, no more setups. No more tagging my photos on Facebook for random suitors back home."

"You and that Facebook. How many months did it take you to remove Steven's photos from your page? And why does your status still say 'in a relationship'?"

"Because I am in a relationship," I declared. "With myself. Best one of my life."

Belinda shook her head. She worried so. It had taken years of excruciating fertility treatments for her to conceive. Six years ago, she became a *manyi*, mother of twins no less, accorded all the respect that was due. To her, my half-*akata* status coupled with a New Yorker's natural independence of spirit had conspired to support a pernicious state of spinsterhood—never mind I was only twenty-nine. Most worryingly, I was childless, an artificial barrenness that, in her view, threatened to be never ending.

"But Chambu—"

"Why can't I find a decent radio station down here?" I jabbed at random preset buttons and happened upon a show promo for some comedian cum disc jockey who'd written a book on "how to find a good man" in response to the supposed dearth of "eligible brothas." Vindicated, Belinda batted my twitchy fingers away from changing the station.

"Phillip's a medical doctor. A ssssurgeon." The last part sounded like a sigh on her lips. Belinda's husband, John, is "merely" a pharmacist, one who'd gone through four grueling years of night school to get his PharmD degree and bragging rights for his wife.

"I've already got a 'Dr.' in front of my name, Bee. I don't need to be Mrs. Dr. So-and-So to feel validated as a human being." I cringed as soon as I said it, though I'd meant every word.

Belinda changed tactics. "He's from our village. Your mom would be so happy."

"Um, I don't think so, cuz. Mom married Anthony Johnson from BK. So, no."

"*Na ya loss, oh!*" she'd fumed, casting a supremely disapproving eye my way as we turned into our driveway, then softly, "I just want you to be happy, Chambu."

"Who says I'm not happy?"

Tuesday, March 1

~~Dear Diary,~~

I'm not happy. In theory, I know that most of these blues are because of my period. Not quite a full stop, but a pause, a comma, in the otherwise contented flow of my life. I know in my head that they come for me the first of each month, unfailingly, like rent due and government checks. I know the whys and the wherefores but they are little comfort when nightmares of crying babies jolt me awake in the middle of the night. My old therapist would remind me to write through my pain and grief. Instead, I'm taking this homeopathic PMS remedy, heinous-tasting SL tabs, to help regulate my "low mood" and "irritability." I had four dissolving under my tongue this afternoon, despite the label's one-a-day proviso. I'd felt no better. The twins cured me somewhat. They are ridiculously upbeat, those two. In bed finally, they wore me out babysitting tonight, but it's a good tired. They did their homework while I did mine—grueling final edits prepping my thesis for publication. God, I wish these academic presses had a real budget. Publisher actually wants me to write a bibliography next but I am so going to farm that out to my TA. Back to the kids: they "helped" prepare dinner, roundly kicked my ass in *Super Mario Kart*, then teased me about it mercilessly as I got them ready for bed. I laughed the first real laugh I'd had in days. I only thought of Steven, of our make-believe baby, once. So dear, darlin', luverly diary, I'm not happy, but I'm getting there.

Wednesday, March 16

Dear ???

Contemplated my chicken salad at lunch and wondered how many Weight Watchers points I racked up. Steven had liked me rounded, fecund. He used to squeeze the rolls of fat on my stomach in satisfaction. Squeezing and squeezing like a stress ball. I'm free to lose that fleshy reminder of him now and Bee swears by WW even though, six years later, she's still carrying some baby weight. I think I've lost a couple of pounds since I got off the pill. I have yet to get on a scale, but I caught Bee eyeing my diminishing derriere in dismay. She said nothing but I knew what she was thinking: *African men like a woman with meat on her bones*—especially below the tailbone. She said nothing, but at dinner I waved her away when she tried to give me seconds, twice.

The Wedding Reception

I am an American, and therefore, a slut.

This universal truth is the basis, in part, for the rumors being spread about me by Catherine and her cabal. Our baby shower showdown has sparked a turf war of sorts between Belinda and her former frenemy. My cousin is furious. There have been glaring face-offs across plastic-covered couches, across backyard barbecues in the boonies, and earlier today, across several church pews as a happy couple exchanged *I do's*.

I find it all curious . . . and slightly hilarious. When Belinda first told me about the gossip, I'd smirked, wondered out loud about the mechanics of being a woman of ill repute. Since I'm only half American, was I only half slut? How did that work, exactly?

Belinda had been less than amused.

This morning, she'd prepared her family for the wedding with the exacting precision of a gendarme general. They wore a uniform: a powder-blue lace attire spun through with gold embroidery for her, a matching *boubou* for her husband, and the children in dark blue with gold accents. She inspected her troops in grim satisfaction as we headed for the car. I was the lone sartorial deserter in a kelly-green sheath and yellow kitten heels.

At the reception now, dancing, I'm glad I wore comfortable shoes. The DJ is playing some old-school *makossa* and *bikutsi* tracks laced with contempo *azonto*. I'm actually having a good time. The uncles who tended to drone on at the mike had miraculously kept their speeches short. There were no snide whispered asides about the bride's recent job loss or the groom's premarital philandering. Even the wedding proper had been nice. I sat through the exchange of vows and felt a sense of reprieve. I can safely attend them now without thinking of Steven and his future wife, the one who'll oh-so-obligingly get pregnant and goose-step with him down the aisle.

An hour later, people are still milling into the hall. Down here it's all about the reception, wedding ceremony optional. I am back at our table sipping a glass of merlot, chatting with Belinda and another tablemate, when I see Catherine Etugebe walk in. For a moment, I watch her unobserved, then take the measure of the man beside her. He is striking. And I am not a woman who is easily struck. Is that Catherine's husband? No—I remember Belinda told me, with savage glee, that Catherine was a wife in name only—not divorced, yet abandoned by her husband for some young *akata* girl. I had held back a chuckle at that. Oh, we *akata* women: home wreckers and slatterns, the lot of us.

"That is Phillip Nyami," says Belinda, catching the direction of my gaze.

His eyes meet mine and linger. His sister notices where he is looking, her mouth an angry slash as she whispers into his ear and pulls him away. He looks back at me once, then again. My face feels flushed. My hand, when I lift up my wineglass, trembles slightly.

"Are you all right? Are you ill? Do you want some *aspreen*?" Bee's accent gets thicker when she worries. Aspirin, in any intonation, is a catchall code for the minipharmacy of analgesics, antipyretics, and

NSAIDs in her voluminous handbag. I give her a weak smile and she pats my hand. "Don't let Cata upset you. She's nothing."

"I'm fine, just fine." Then turning to our tablemate, "Uncle, what were you saying about tax annuities again?"

For the next thirty minutes, I listen to the intricacies of the tax code absentmindedly before Belinda excuses us to escape to the ladies' room. Except for my flush, there is a blessed silence within the cloister of these porcelain walls. Belinda is touching up her war paint at the mirror when Catherine Etugebe marches in with one of her brigade.

"*How na, manyi?*" Catherine says the last word with emphasis, a sneering salute. The latest volley in her campaign of intimidation: telling all and sundry that Belinda is a "fake" *manyi*—pumped up on drugs to produce a multiple birth à la Octomom. "*She be nah one for talk,*" Belinda had said. "All her own babies, *dey for inside toilet.*"

"*How na, small?*" Belinda retorts, her last word recalling the other woman's former junior status as her "little sister" at the elite girls' boarding school they both attended back in Cameroon.

I stand next to my cousin and the other woman stands next to Catherine, trying to give me a menacing stare but failing woefully due to a lazy left eye.

Catherine cuts her eyes at me. "*How na, akata gal?*"

Enough is enough. This is one of those moments I wish I was more like my dad's side of the family. I'd be taking my earrings off and getting the Vaseline. Instead I'm an academic, trained to use my words, so with icy enunciation, I say, "Hello to you too, Catherine and co." Head nod to her friend. "I was just telling Belinda what a good time I'm having. How welcome everyone has made me feel since I moved to DC. You know how it is when you move to a new place, *some* people can be so cliquish and insecure, so juvenile."

I smile.

It is not a nice smile.

"*Akata. No try me, oh! You wan begin look at ma brotha—*"

Belinda huffs, "Cata! *No try me—you no knowsay shoulder no di eva pass head?*" Belinda shouts. "*Who be you? You thinksay you better pass*

all man cuz ya papa na bigshot minister for Cameroon! Big compound,
big moto, so what? We dey we for America. For America, Cata Etugebe na
secretary! Chambu, we di go we."

And with that parting shot, we storm out of the bathroom and make
it halfway down the hallway before erupting into giggles. Just like that
we are twelve years old again, taking on the neighborhood bully side by
side. I miss feeling this close to her.

"Belinda, you should have seen your face . . ." I'm gasping and gig-
gling, clutching my stomach.

"Me? Chambu, I thought you were going to slap her when she called
you *akata gal.*"

"It was close there for a second, Bee." I loop her arm with mine.
"Come on. Let's go have some fun. You go dance with that handsome
husband of yours, and—"

"And you go hear more about tax loopholes."

Fifteen minutes later, Belinda is on the dance floor with John,
the kids are running around playing with other children, and Phillip
Nyami is watching me. I refuse to turn and look, but the feeling of his
eyes on my body is exquisite.

"Is someone sitting here?" His voice is not quite as deep as I thought
it would be, but it's still very pleasant with a slight accent.

"No, go right ahead and sit, young man," says my tablemate and
self-appointed tax adviser.

"I'm Phillip." He takes the chair right next to mine. A hair's breadth
away; I can see freckles on the bridge of his nose.

"I know who you are."

"Yes." He gives a knowing smile. "I believe you met my sister."

"I'm not quite sure *met* is the right word for it." My smile, an echo
of his.

"Encountered?"

"Nope."

"Came across?"

"Not quite."

"Bumped into?"

"Ballpark. How about *collided, clashed*?"

"How about we meet and start fresh? Just you and me. Pretend our relatives haven't told us everything they think they know about us." He leans into me, takes my hand. "Hello, I'm Phillip."

"I'm Genevieve."

"Pleased to meet you, luv. Heard through the grapevine that you're new in town."

"British!"

"Huh?"

"Your accent. I've been trying to place it."

"Nice one. I grew up in Brixton."

"Oh, are you just here for the wedding?" Is that disappointment in my voice? Weird.

"No, no. I'm in finance. My company just transferred me here from our London offices."

"London, I've always wanted to go. But I've been on a ramen noodles budget the past few years, with grad school and all."

"Grad school?"

"Anthropology. I'm an anthropologist."

"You must really enjoy this, then." He sweeps his hand to encompass the circle of dancers forming on the floor as the DJ switches to a ceremonial bottle dance. "Come on, let's soak up the 'musical traditions of the grassland peoples of Cameroon.'" The last bit cheekily delivered in a Herzog documentary drawl.

"I'm not *that* kind of anthropologist," I say archly, even as I allow him to take my hand and lead me to the dance floor.

Five songs later, we are still on the floor. There's a drop of sweat rolling down my chest in time with the *thump, thump, thump* of a reggae beat. I feel the weight of several stares on us and I don't care. It is the first time in a long time that my body has felt wholly my own. I feel wanton, like a Mami Wata, like the fallen woman I've been proclaimed to be. I turn around and fit my backside into the groove of Phillip's body.

"My sister warned me about the dangers of American girls." His voice is whispery against the coil of my ear. He pulls me close.

"Did she now?" I smile at him over my shoulder as I settle into him. I may only be half American, but I rub that half against him for all I'm worth.

Friday, April 29

~~Dear Journal 'o' mine,~~

Home. I need a home of my own. Since the wedding reception I'd been seeing Phillip, first in my dreams, then in person. The first few weeks were filled with infrequent sightings: like glimpses of a yeti, the Loch Ness monster, or the unicorn of my girlhood diary. There he is at the buffet table at a cousin's graduation party and there again at a recital. After the third sighting he asked me for my number. Since the fourth, we've been like teenagers: long phone calls and necking at the back of parties while our loved ones continue their standoff. I need a home of my own. A love shack. The contractors hit some gas main while tearing through the walls now, so I'm in for further delays. I don't drive. New Yorker, here. We live too far out to catch a Metro. I've resorted to peeking at Belinda's calendar and creating a time line of places where Phillip and I can meet. Tomorrow, it's a funeral.

The Memorial Service

At the *cry-dies* back home they have professional keeners—women who, for a nominal fee, will blubber and produce high-pitched wails on cue. I am sure it's not completely disingenuous. I imagine that in small villages there must be some point of connection, however distant. A cousin of a friend of the teacher who knew the deceased. I imagine they must have some touchstone, some place deep down inside they access to draw forth the requisite sadness. Like an actor getting into character, they find their motivation—a lost love, a found love that went sour. They find that one hurt to make the tears, when they do come, real.

"Papa God, we knowsay you di make a way where way no dey. We knowsay you be Alpha and Omega. Through you all things dey possible," the Nigerian pastor intones in pidgin, his words in a language we all can understand—prayer.

Mr. Elias Fonchuak's memorial service is a small one. It turns out his family had paid the exorbitant price to ship their loved one's body to be buried on his native soil. At age seventy-two, Mr. Fonchuak made the same trip back home he had every other year in life. On this last and final journey, he traveled in the plane's cargo hold instead of an economy-class window seat. Belinda tells me he was laid to rest in the village with all the attendant rites and rituals for funerals. The delegations of mourners from various tribal constituencies. Drumming, dancing, and blowing of horns. Plenty *chop*, plenty *mimbo*: libations of palm wine, Guinness, Heineken, and 33 Export. Yet despite the pomp and circumstance, all the public fanfare, I find funerals back home intimate. Mr. Fonchuak's family had the chance to wash his body, to dress him in his favorite suit themselves, to lay him out in a coffin in their own parlor. They had the chance to really say goodbye. A chance to mourn.

A chance I never had with my own baby when she died.

"Papa God, you be talksay 'ashes to ashes dust to dust.' We dey here for this life only at your mercy."

"You killed my baby." Those were some of the last words Steven ever said to me.

Have mercy.

I was hitting him before I even realized. Arms flailing.

"Don't you dare! Don't you fucking dare blame this on me!" But hadn't I already questioned myself? Hadn't I wondered if I'd been working too hard? If I'd been eating right?

Steven grabbed my arms and, none too gently, he shook me.

"You are sick, you know that? What woman, what *real* woman, doesn't want to have a baby?"

This negro. Throwing that in my face then. In our early days, I'd made the mistake of telling Steven that sometimes I was terrified of pregnancy, of growing huge and immobile, beached by my own body. I craved movement and momentum in my life. He had teased me then, held me, joked about saving money to travel to Gujarat like we'd read about in the *Times*—a place where entire villages of Indian women were renting their wombs. It was all a joke till I got my fellowship. *It's only a year*, I told him. *A lot can happen in a year. I don't want us to fall apart*, he replied. There were tears from me, lots of angst from him, then suddenly everything was fine. He was his cheery, optimistic self again. And me? I was getting plump.

I didn't think anything of it at first. I was on the pill. My weight always fluctuated. I always ate when I was stressed. I was tired a lot, but assumed it was just the pressure of getting ready to travel, finishing my thesis, the relationship. I assumed a lot till a thin blue line told me otherwise.

"Steven, I'm pregnant," I blurted out at dinner one night. I hadn't told him for a month; now I had spurted it out over dim sum. I hadn't told anyone, not even Belinda. I don't think I could have borne her joy. Instead I had started writing it all down.

Steven dropped his chopsticks.

"Finally," he said. This look came over his face then. It wasn't surprise, it was something akin to relief.

"Finally?" I echoed weakly.

"I mean, it's just so great. Finally, we can really be together. Really get on with our lives without all the distractions."

I saw something in him then, something sly, slithery.

I said nothing for the rest of dinner at Hai Fu's Kitchen, nothing in the ride back to our apartment, nothing until we were alone in bed together that night. Steven had been carrying on a one-man conversation filled with plans—with BabyBjörns, day rompers, night rompers, and Diaper Genies.

I turned to him. Palmed his face with both hands.

"Steven, I want you to be absolutely honest with me. What did you mean when you said 'finally'?"

Steven was a terrible liar. It was one of the things I had loved about him. He was too good a man to be too good at deception. But that slithery look came again. It took an hour, but he told me everything. The solicitousness—the maraschino cherry ice cream, the hour-long foot massages whenever he thought it was time for my cycle. He'd been monitoring me, my fertility, and tampering with my birth control. There were tears again, lots of angst again as well. *I just didn't want to lose you, baby,* he'd said. *Lose me, you're going to lose more than me when I get an abortion!* But even as I said the words, I knew they weren't true. I was so angry with Steven at that moment, but not angry enough to kill our child. Even as much as I hated him right then, I stayed. I was in love. I was terrified. What was I going to do about my life, my fellowship, my graduate work?

Four months into my pregnancy with my daughter, the baby we had decided to name Belinda, Mother Nature answered all my questions for me. I miscarried. When I told Steven, some of the last words he ever said to me:

"What woman, what *real* woman, doesn't want a baby?"

"Maybe it's just your baby. Maybe I don't want your 'special delivery,'" I said, knowing this would wound Steven—a postal worker, a man who'd worried I would someday outgrow him. "Maybe I just didn't want to have a baby with you."

He shook me then, again, then again, and again, and again.

For months after, I'd been filled with nothing but rage. But I understand him better now. His grief, his need to lash out, his lazy need to place blame. I understand now, but I still can't forgive.

"Papa God, as we di mourn your son, we knowsay he dey for your side, he dey for heaven."

I think of my baby Belinda in heaven and I am crying. Teary-faced mourners look at me in sympathy, no doubt thinking how beloved Mr. Fonchuak was by all. I think only of my baby girl and begin sobbing in earnest, my face in my hands. Belinda is rubbing my shoulders. They shake with the force of my grief. From somewhere I feel a strong hand at my back, turning me into an even stronger shoulder. I look up. Phillip. He has come to me, oblivious to the stares. The whispers now.

I put my head on his shoulder and settle into him.

Friday, May 13
Dear Belinda,

My darling baby girl. I am finally in my own home, with my own bed. I feel like you are watching over me now. But try not to watch too hard when Phillip comes over tomorrow night. Before I left her home, Bee told me she felt like she was losing me. I knew she was talking about more than just the move. There was a distance between us. We had come a long way from those little girls who dreamed together, who spoke pidgin English as a secret language in the make-believe kingdoms only the two of us shared. I have kept a lot of secrets from her, secrets like you. When I told her about you, she was wounded. Hurt by my silence on something so dear, then I told her your name. We are not what we once were but we are getting there.

It's quiet here tonight. So empty my voice echoes. Sometimes I holler just to hear it bounce off the walls. I don't mind being alone so much now. I hug myself, grab hold of my chest, my arms, my persistent pooch, and take comfort in the feeling of my own flesh and blood.

The Living Infinite

Since the death of her husband Nala has felt at sea. Memories are rare pearls sifted from the silt of her grief. She remembers years as a youngling raised on the shores of an African land. Portuguese explorer Fernando Pó had named it for the spectral crustaceans flitting forth from sandy burrows, mating in opal lagoons, for days on end. In the sun-dappled throes of their ecstasy, they made easy, and quite tasty, prey. Secreted away in the shade of mangroves, Nala would cleave open their porcelain shells, reveling in the burst of salt and zesty life as her tongue dove into the sweetly tender morsels of flesh within.

Her most recent memories flow from the bayous and wetlands of Louisiana, home to her late husband of forty-five years, Byron. The night she met him was a watershed moment of which, if one embraces life in all its complexities, there are sure to be many. Especially for one such as she who has lived to the ripe young age of 202.

• • •

Across a humid bar, in a beachside gazebo, set so close to the shore that the pounding of the soukous beat nearly rivaled the din of crashing surf, Byron laid eyes on her. He was all *fiya*-burn and swagger, ordering a grasshopper for the lady "in the coral dress" without so much as a *bonsoir, chérie*. And though she was a whiskey-neat woman, Nala wasn't one to turn down a complimentary cocktail or the good-looking man bold enough to buy it. Full of big dreams and sweeping plans, the *akata* was nothing like the *ton-tons* of her sleepy waterfront town or even the big shots she bedded in the bustling port town of Douala. The hunt grew new to her. *HER*. A Mami Wata. A seasoned seducer of thousands of men, now made eager and shy, trembling as he took her hand. She thrilled to it. As they danced hip to hip, she inhaled an intoxicating mixture of clean mint, briny sweat, and something unknowable that reminded her of whale song and undertows and dark ocean depths where there be monsters.

As he walked her home later, she noted that he'd grown solemn. Perhaps wondering where his night would end—by her doorstep or her bedside. She was wondering herself. She would fuck him silly of course, but the rest, this strange need to hear him talk, to smell the crème de menthe on the tip of his tongue. *What was that?* She was damned if she knew. Seeking answers, she began the first of that night's several tests. Ordering him the tasty fried grasshoppers she loved to munch on after an evening out.

"Taste this," Nala demanded, pressing a small brown packet from a street vendor into Byron's waiting palm, even as she pressed the first mystery bite to his lips.

She watched him take a tentative nibble, chew contemplatively, taking his sweet, sweet time.

"Well? Say something! Do you like it?"

"It's pretty good. *Très bon*. What is it?"

"A local delicacy—fried grasshopper." And she waited. For the spit take. For the frown.

"Well, damn!" he said, smiling. "You're already halfway to being a bayou girl. When you come visit me, I'll cook you up some 'gator and frog legs."

Ha! She laughed and whirled around in a little jig. Went keeling into him. Dizzy. Like she'd swum up to the surface too fast. Her soul effervesced. *Was this "happy"?*

. . .

"Would you like it?" he asked her later still. He was standing behind her, hands surfing the crest of her hip bones in a teasing grip. The evening's gloam shadowed his words, casting them against the bare walls, against her bare back.

"*Like* weti?" She smiled coyly in the dark, her forehead joining her palms to rest against the concrete wall, a cool respite in her sweltering bedroom. "What is it you think I need, *Monsieur* Stillwater? I have sunshine and music and the ocean vast. That's more than enough for me."

"Would you like something more?" he asked. "An adventure? A love? Would you like to be my woman?" Those words, whispered into the shell of her ear, somehow felt beyond her, an eternity away, a mirage on a distant horizon.

"Foolish man," she said. "Be serious. *Habi* you drank too much Guinness and palm wine tonight?"

In answer, he licked a wet groove up the Gaboon viper tattoo slithering along the column of Nala's spine, sidling round the curve of her ribs, then the conch shell of a breast, the poison pink of a forked tongue coiled around an areola, fangs bared. Byron bit her nipple. She shuddered. Her mind whirled ahead with the complications and the *this-can't-be*'s till the very moment he fit himself to her backside, pushing past parted thighs to stroke that sweetly tender spot again and again and again, so that moments later she would cry out *yes* and know she was ready for anything and everything.

. . .

The wedding of Byron Thelonious Stillwater to Nala Wouri DeCamaroes was officiated by Reverend Dr. Felix Tidwell III at St. Augustine's

Church in the Tremé, New Orleans. Of the 126 guests throwing bird-seed on the church steps, dancing in the brass band's second line, or later supping on shrimp and grits, oyster bisque, *paupiette de poulet*, and bananas Foster, all 126 were friends and family and a grudgingly invited colleague, or two, of the groom. At the reception, the bride delivered heartfelt regrets on behalf of her family, which was admittedly diminutive—no living parents, just three sisters—in comparison to the groom's booming clan. So many had made the trip, special, up from Pointe à la Hache way down there in Plaquemines Parish. But the bride's people were back in Africa, and that's a long, long ways away. So there's that.

"*Putain*, I hate those broke-foot bitches!" This was Nala to her newly minted husband in the limo to the reception, where 126 guests, none of whom were the twenty-three female sister-cousins from around the globe she had actually invited, waited to fete them. "Not one word from them—no RSVP, no nothing. *Connasses!*"

It was not in her nature to cry, but she felt her pupils kerning her eyes to full-on eel black, so she turned to her husband and let him see her in full fury. Reminded him, poor human man, what he was getting himself into.

"Now don't go giving me the evil eye, *chérie*. Family is what you make it, and like it or not you've got me now." He planted the wettest of smooches right on her cheek. "It's a 'thick and thin' type thing."

And then he tickled her, roaming his hands up inside her fishtail wedding dress so that they had to tell the driver to circle the hall ~~one, two,~~ four times so a shirttail could get tucked in, that garter put to rights, but where were her—*never mind, we're late enough, let's just go in.*

The entire reception, while Nala danced and twirled under the glow of Baccarat chandeliers, Byron smiled and grinned wide and every once in a while had a hearty belly chuckle as he flicked his fingertips along the lacy frill of his wife's silk panties, balled to a nubbin in his right front pocket.

● ● ●

Dawns at sea on the Stillwater family boats were Nala's favorite—quixotic, mystical. Byron was born to a seafaring clan that had made their living harvesting shrimp and oysters and all manner of water creatures in the Gulf for generations on end. He had grown up fishing with his father on weekends and summers. And when her schedule swim-coaching Ninth Ward youth and his busy maritime law practice allowed it, they still went down together for two of four weekends each month.

She was a quick-study deckhand: listening keenly for the hollow echo a dead oyster made when she *tap-tap* tested its shell with the blunt end of her hatchet. Spot-on in sorting out spat—oyster younglings—to rebed for future harvests. On the docks, she was schooled by O.G. skippers. Grizzled and gray men who taught her how to shuck an oyster, seed its beds, build a reef, work a dredge, and the dying skill of weaving its intricate nets by hand—knitting even-steven squares at just the width of her ring and middle fingers twined together.

On all of her husband's boats—the trawler, the lugger, even the wooden skiff she'd painted a Day-Glo green mimicking the bioluminescent kelp of her home waters—she scribed poetry, or runes, or nautical quotes, or rough translations of the clicking dolphin-speak passed down from her mother. *KK-kkkk-KKKKKKKK-kk*—you are my heart song.

She wished her sister-cousins could see these shimmering waters at dawn, hear the kazoo chortles of its gulls, inhale the rich ambrosia of her husband's piping-hot coffee, hot-water cornbread, and hominy grits cut with honey. Wished they could release their tight clutch on the old ways and try to fathom the truth of her union. But they distrusted man as a rule and men particularly on principle. Men carried harpoons. Men hunted your sisters to adorn the palaces of their capricious kings. Men offered shiny baubles if only you'd cut your fins. That she had married one. A fishmonger? *A fisherman*, she'd corrected, then corrected herself: *a maritime attorney*. A what? *A lawyer for the sea*. Hmph—what do fish need man's law for? If there's trouble, we take to the tides.

And such had been her own life for more than a hundred years—beached on the shores of foremothers who took to the sea soon after their girl-children grew breasts—no longer their babes but newborn Mami Watas. Her clan were nomads, explorers, sea gypsies. They settled on no land. They took a man for the pleasure of it and for the *gris-gris* it gave—longevity, strength, youth. They had no need of life mates. They made friends with sharks.

• • •

A Mami Wata's essence is moonlight and desire melded to one. Nala knows this in her marrow, in her fins. Lasirèn, Yemanja, Oxum, Erzulie, Jine-Faro, Santa Marta. Their bloodline flowed through miles of sandy lagoons and tidal estuaries along Africa's coastline. In her homeland, Nala's clanswomen are worshipped as goddesses till this day, queen of queens reigning on high in a pantheon of *miengu*, wanton water deities. They are the descendants of Mojili, a spirit-ruler hailing from a time before man, her name so powerful, so revered, it could not be uttered before small children lest they perish. Mothers plunged ailing *pickin* into the *miengu's* healing waters, would-be mothers bathed in their streams, cupping mystic pools in their palms, hoping one day to conceive. Fleets of supplicant fishermen in dugout canoes prayed for a good catch overflowing with ghost shrimp or pygmy herring or butter catfish. They made offerings of things that tinkled and the shiny trifles *miengu* adored: jeweled hairpins, *shine-shine* looking glasses, even impudent timepieces daring to measure the long spell of their lives.

While Nala fully embraced her new existence, her true nature was never quelled. She and her clanswomen were jealous ones. Oft demanding adoration, quick to dole out stern correction to a foolishly fickle man who might be shown the error of his ways when his home burned to ashes, as his business loans went forfeit, or when a walk in tall grass sliced through skin and tendon like a verdant scalpel. Her kin ridiculed sisters in distant climes, ones whose harum-scarum hearts had swept them off course. Ones who let themselves be bogged down by litters of leaky-nosed mouth breathers. Captives in nets of their own design.

• • •

"Another man?" Nala took a deep breath she had no need of. It was a mirroring of her landlocked tribesmen she had first begun long ago to blend in. To express emotions as they. Like sorrow. It was second nature now. Another breath.

"Another man?" she said, repeating her husband's words in the dark. He was stroking her hair. Fanning it across the bed pillow, strands gilded silver in the moonlight. There was a sadness about his eyes. She had never before been with a man long enough to see it. *Worry.*

"Trust me. I am more than satisfied," she assured him.

He gave a deep chuckle. Pushed his swelling hardness against her thigh. "Oh, I know. But you need more than good dick, *chérie*. You need magic."

He buried his face in her hair. Breathing deep.

And though what he was saying was true. Though she had probably cut her lifespan by more than a century just to be loyal to him. She stroked his hair and told him another kind of truth. "You and I, my love. We make our own juju."

"You sure?" he asked, voice muffled in her hair.

Was she? What did she know of the human heart? She knew she had surprised him at the office for lunch one day. Had seen a redheaded paralegal temp perched atop his desk, her skirt riding skyward. She knew she had cornered the woman in the executive bathroom. Had ever so sweetly suggested she find new employ. Then not so sweetly rewarded the woman's backtalk by slamming her against a tiled wall. The sudden roar and heat of a hand dryer had startled them both. Love was a thing with claws. This she knew.

He lifted his head. She swiped moisture from his lashes.

"I'm sure," she told him.

• • •

In her true form, Nala races fleet-finned marlins and wins. She could hold her breath for up to an hour—awing pearl hunters free-diving bare-skinned like the Ama women in Wajima City and the Haenyo ladies on Jeju Island. Few things scared her. Some troubled waters haunted her. On their jubilee anniversary, a celebratory transatlantic cruise was cut short because her nightly swim left her in tears, triggered nightmares of chains and people screaming in tongues from back home.

But the time she was truly fearful was on their first night together, when she let Byron see her truly naked. Her final test.

"Close your eyes," she told him, as she rose up from the bed, draping its sheet around her. Byron lay there, stretched out and unabashedly nude.

He tugged the trailing hem of the sheet.

"Little too late for that. Don't you think?" He ducked the tissue box she halfheartedly threw. "I've already seen all the goods."

"No. You haven't—"

"Well, unless I missed something in health class—"

"It's no sickness. I want you to see me. *Fermez tes yeux.*"

"You want to play, *ma chérie*?" He chuckled darkly, then placed a hand over his eyes. "Let's play."

"No peeking," she said, letting the change ripple through her.

She drew nearer, put her hand over his own, then let the sheet drop. She placed his other hand on her transformed thigh, moving his fingertips along its scales.

"What do you feel?"

"Something hard but supple. Like a shell, with a heartbeat. What *is* that?"

"Wait," she said, as he made to uncover his eyes. "And this?"

She ran his fingers along the tiny fins that covered her forearms like fine down.

He pushed her hand away. "It's you. All you."

"It's me."

She stood silent as the deep. Letting him look over her. Watched his eyes coast over the indigo-trellised gold scales plating her hips and thighs, glimmering like blue-ray limpets in strong flows. Taking his sweet, molasses-drip time to take it all in—from her feather-fine fins to the gills at her breastbone. She knew this might be too much to absorb, even with her full form yet unveiled. But still.

She thought she knew what forever felt like.

"Well, say something, idiot!" She couldn't cry, but her eyes were near to changing and giving this man one more reason to run just as she was telling herself to *let him run, I don't care.*

"So you're a Maman Dlo." He smiled. "Goddamn, I must be a lucky man!"

And then he was hugging her close and telling her of his people, of Orisha water deities—spirits that kept them safe, that blessed them with a bountiful catch.

And that was that.

• • •

She had always believed that water would be the death of him. Through the years, she gave him as much of her *gris-gris* as she could, to keep him strong, to keep him safe. FUN FACT: According to the CDC, commercial fishing consistently ranks as one of the most dangerous occupations in America.

"Gray hairs! See this? You're giving me gray hairs!" She was letting herself age so they could grow old together, staring incredulously at her fresh-faced husband as she grabbed his unlined visage between her cool palms, swiveling his head to and fro. "So you want to drive me to a nursing home while you visit me with your new wife? *Which kind juju this?*"

"It's that old black magic," he said. "We humans of a darker hue like to say 'Black don't crack.'" He laughed. "We say it's the melanin but it's really something else. We got that soul glow-up," and with this he burst into a ditty from *Coming to America*, "Just let your soul glow!" Drawing out the *soul* into ten falsetto syllables, drawing his wife to him till she grumpily unfolded the arms locked over her chest and let him hug the ever-loving life out of her, saying, "I'll get you some Clairol for them grays, *ma chouchoute*."

"Gray hairs!" she screeched whenever he crewed with friends on a strange boat whose seaworthiness was unknown to her. She would leave clipped *Times-Picayune* articles on fishing-related accidents and stats on crewmen who fell overboard around their home.

But he always came home safe and sound.

Then came Hurricane Katrina. Disruption. Destruction. Despair. The Big Easy took a bruising.

What else can be said that is not already known? The Superdome. The rooftop riders. The floating bodies. The hopelessness. The relief then shame at the snatch of joy when your own high-ground home was spared. The homes of others, in fact their very lives, seemingly so expendable. When water bloat burst the levees, they had been relatively safe. The week prior, Byron had stocked their pantry with emergency supplies—fresh water, batteries, frozen food, and garbage pails of water. The generator was operational. Her saltwater ground pool was level.

They watched the news as water came pouring through the Seventeenth Street Canal, Lake Pontchartrain rushing into the bell jar of the city. At home, their windows rattled, driving rain shook the trees like frenzied pompoms. The streets went slick with wet.

Tens upon tens of thousands trapped. Drowning in their very homes.

They took Byron's boat out to help. The water she loved a *cauchemar*, a brackish gumbo of human remains and soggy belongings. She dove deep, again and again, swimming into homes submerged like so much sunken treasure. Searching and searching for the most elusive of treasures: survivors. They spied a teddy bear floating near a treetop, were in tears when they found its owner, lil' bit that she was, clinging somehow to a branch. Trip after trip, picking up the stranded, listening as shell-shocked voices told them of evacuation, of bridge crossings on foot, of warning shots to turn back. So many missing. So much sorrow. It seemed second nature to humans.

Nala took a deep breath.

Later, they would rebuild. So too, the city. Albeit slowly.

But then a *Deepwater Horizon* oil rig on the BP-owned pipeline in the Macondo Prospect (imagine that, named for Gabo's benighted town) exploded and spent eighty-seven days gushing 210 million gallons of crude oil into the Gulf of Mexico. Nala cried for days. Sickened by the sight of gulls covered in its slick, of fish choking on tar balls. Always oil, always *wahala*! When oil was found along her old home shores, nations had nearly gone to war to claim the area, ousting Bakassi villagers from their homes, from ancestral fishing grounds. Now her husband was making himself heartsick (high blood pressure ran in his family, so they missed the truth of it) with the number of civil cases he took on seeking restitution. Trying to right things that would never be the same again. *Breathe, Nala. Breathe.*

But he took his heart pills and regained a little of his ceaseless hope when he won his clients some money against Big Oil. He prevailed.

Water did get him in the end, though. At sixty-five, after sniffling and sneezing and nursing a cold for five days, Byron Thelonious Stillwater collapsed and was rushed to Tulane Medical Center where he died four days later of acute pneumonia complicated by pulmonary edema. Water in the lungs.

"I am not calling this a home-going ceremony," Nala shouted. "Not a 'home going' or a 'send-off' or any other bullshit. He's not on vacation. My man is dead! He's dead!"

Her parlor room was filled with Byron's many solicitous aunties. One held her now, rocking her and saying, "Yes, baby. Let it all out."

"I just couldn't," Nala kept on, gulping breaths she didn't need, shedding tears she did, buoyed by the woman's sturdy shoulder. "I couldn't stick him in the ground neither!"

"Yes, baby."

"Water—"

"Yes, chile. Anything you want. Anything." The aunty held a glass of water to Nala's parched lips.

"His life was the water," said Nala, between reluctant sips. "That's where he belongs for whatever comes next."

For days, she was dry-eyed. Waves of grief had swelled in and over her, receding just long enough for the odd phone call to be made arranging flowers and harpists. And for her family to be notified that their presence in Louisiana was, once again, being requested. A handful of its various members had maintained an anemic and desultory connection with her through the years by way of Facebook and the occasional bits of correspondence. But now, at least three of her twenty-three sister-cousins were present. They were open to change, these younglings, unfettered by the trawls of tradition.

Byron's acid-tongued centurion *grand-mère*, *Maman* Lulu, was grumbling under her breath in guttural Creole, making sure the whole room knew, in no uncertain terms, what she thought of these Janie-come-lately sisters and what they could go do with themselves. "*Voilà merde! Nala! Di 'kasse twah' a ton salluh famille des cochons!*"

Family.

Her sister-cousins: Marie-Francoise, a melusine living along the coast of France, was stretched out on a chaise eating bon-bons. Coira, a selkie who lived part of her life as a harp seal, looked jumpy and restless on a corner divan. Only Helena, a siren whose foremothers had taken a particular interest in luring men to their deaths, was able to say anything meaningful on the subject of last rites.

"In the old countries, families would send the man they lost out to sea on his craft. Set aflame, so his ashes would become one with the ocean waves."

"I think ye'll be needing permits for that in this country," said Coira, pushing her slipping tortoiseshell glasses from the cliff of her nose.

"Are there more bon-bons?" asked Marie-Francoise from her cushiony velveteen swoon.

Nala turned to her and hissed. "They're in the cupboard, next to my dead husband's ashes," she spat out. "Ask me about bon-bons again. I dare you."

Just then *Maman* Lulu burst out into such a rib-tickled fit of laughter that soon the whole room was cackling along with her, clutching their sides and letting out the occasional toot, or two.

• • •

Family.

The Stillwaters gone for the evening. Nala's sistren gathered close.

"*Soit-pas malheureuse, grand-sœur,*" Marie-Francoise chided. "You are a tough one. Not soft like me, eh?" She pushed Nala's fingers into the dimpled flesh of her forearm, then handed her a packet. "Homemade truffles—*avec chocolat.* To remind you life will be sweet again."

Coira shuffled over with travel brochures, handing them to Nala with a plane ticket, babbling: "When ye're lonesome, come visit Strandhill. My husband, Seamus, makes a mean bowl of poundies: the freshest potatoes, hot butter, all the fixings. We'll eat it with cockles picked fresh off the beach, we will. Listen to me. Rabbiting on and on, amn't I? My husbands always say—"

"Husbands?" Helena asked, accustomed to keeping her own legions of men well accounted for.

Coira breathily explained her land and sea marriages to two males: Ossian, selkie himself, and Seamus, a human. She was blushing all the while. More so when Helena exclaimed: "So the little seal has secrets.

See, Nala, you see? There is always love to be had. When you are ready, you and I we will take my Adolpho's yacht sailing. We will sample the *malakas* in Mykonos and Santorini and Crete."

"*Putain!*" Nala burst out laughing. "Helena, you are too much."

• • •

In the end, Nala Wouri DeCamaroes Stillwater spread her dearheart Byron Thelonious Stillwater's ashes on Barataria Bay, the waters of his forefathers down in Plaquemines Parish. The farewell service was officiated by Reverend Dr. Felix Tidwell IV of the Tremé, New Orleans. Of the sixty guests throwing magnolias over the boat railing, fifty-seven were friends and family of the Stillwaters. A harpist played in the background as each person read out quotes that Mrs. Stillwater had scribed on her dearly departed's boats through the years.

> *I am not tragically colored. There is no great sorrow dammed up in my soul, nor lurking behind my eyes. . . . I do not weep at the world—I am too busy sharpening my oyster knife.*
> —ZORA NEALE HURSTON

> *The sea is only the embodiment of a supernatural and wonderful existence. It is nothing but love and emotion; it is the 'Living Infinite.'*
> —JULES VERNE

A day later, another farewell, in Nala's NOLA backyard. Four women—a Mami Wata, a melusine, a selkie, and a siren—made their way into moonlight. Skyclad. Naked footfalls muted by dew-stroked grass. Wading into the warm waters of a pool, they let the change come over them, one by one by one by one. Four creatures swam. Fin to flipper. They floated. Eyes tugged skyward. Scales laid bare. Nala opened her throat to give voice to her farewell, ululating with her sister-cousins, their fin song rising to join the chorus of cicadas, a slow and strange dirge reminiscent of whale song in somber seas. Barely clinging to the heavens, the moon hung low and full. Nala waxed and waned by its leave, its lush hush pressed upon her, waiting on something, her howl perhaps. Quick as a whirlpool, she whipped her caudal fin beneath her, propelled upward with such force that agitated water roiled below. Nala hung in the stars for a moment, wild hair blotting out the moon, closer to heaven and her love.

Fin

Kinks

Relaxed

They descended as one. Lying in wait at the 125th Street subway exit, they were legion, scent coming to her on a cold gust of air, clot thick with crayfish, cracked asphalt fumes, and blue hair grease. They were three, no six, now eight African hair braiders, a bulwark of *ankara* head ties and fleshy, bangled arms blocking her way. Neon flyers outstretched and at the ready. Theirs the bright fluorescent smiles of big-box store greeters: artificial, flickering, gone. Voices cried out, "Sista, sista, sista. We give you good style, good price." Moving ever closer, cutting off egress to the snow-banked sidewalks and wintry world beyond.

Jennifer Tchandep tensed at their approach, self-consciously raising a hand to her own relaxed strands, extending the other to palm three, then four, urgently bestowed business cards, smile hard-edged as she knifed through their fold. A nearby trash can caught her eye but theirs were on her still, so she tucked down her head, moving onward. She walked down an embassy row of beauty care shops: Dominican *pelo* salons, South Asian eyebrow threaders, and Korean beauty supplies purveying *its mine 'cause I bought it* hair—human, synthetic, prepacked, or by the pound, colors rainbowing from acid-green ombré to #60's icy blond, flowing bone straight or deeply twisting, with a

155

yin-yang of stickered prices, showcasing fire sales on Indian Remy and sky-high markups on virgin Brazilian.

Jennifer's toes were steeped in wet, high-heeled suede boots ruined now. Each step sinking them deeper into the snow-swaddled treacheries of the Harlem streets: the crooked, bottle-shard grins of last night's stoop revelries, the gnawed bones and fatty-rind discards of sated people, the crumpled flyers extolling the virtues of Falani's shea butter—homemade and small batched, ancient properties prized by dusky Nubian queens—now available to you and yours for just $5.99.

She rested against the flaking-paint dandruff of a lamppost, adjusting the heft of the manuscript in her arms. Poorly bound, it had chafed through her light coat for three blocks, but she'd kept walking, seeking distance and solitude. Steady now. Breathing deep. Icicled air whistling through the deep caverns of her lungs. Damn, the women had startled her. Last night, she had shed her city skin, left its prickly-pear alertness between Egyptian cotton sheets. She felt raw, all laid bare, shivering in the tongue-ripened flesh her lover had licked and bitten till dawn, leaving her dazed and unaware of the world and its specters. Till now.

She discarded the flyers, the cards, in movements both guilty and surreptitious. Those poor braiders, she thought, working 25/8, all walk-in comers welcome, so many asylum seekers fleeing war zones and other savagery she could never fathom. For them, America might never be a land of milk and honey, their dreams curdling, life-sapping hours spent hunched over this client, then that client, then another other client's crown. She had watched silently, complicit, as braiders rubbed and rubbed the rictus of sore, creaking fingers, had heard their stories piecemeal, in salons or in public television excerpts revealing a litany of village outrages: gun-toting sons in threadbare camo, other sons trekking in the dust and dark, penned in cages for their own protection. Like other Americans, she had borne witness to these quotidian horrors telescoped from afar. At times, she wished she could unknow, unsee. A disgusting frailty, yes, she knows, especially because she's supposed to be African too, isn't she? Sometimes in bed, in the deep velvet of night, she shuts her eyes tight and makes herself see, lets the images linger across the dark theater of her lids, glimpses hut-bound relatives whose woes by birthright should have been known to her, as intimate as a child's prayers whispered, or a blow—quick and hard-knuckled—from a lover spurned.

Braided

Prodigal sons and daughters of the diaspora—brought to this nation in chaos and chains, so many still shackled in prisons of the mind and the state. Emancipate yourselves! Return to the welcoming bosom of the African motherland. Go home to a place where Black lives ALWAYS matter. You may be ill-equipped for that physical journey, crippled— financially, emotionally—by the very nation that you wet- nursed and laid bricks for, the very society that would sooner gun you down than give you a job. But I'm here to tell you that you are ready, that we all can make that spiritual pil- grimage. Make that reconnection to what the unenlightened call primitive because they, in their false supremacy, privi- lege the almighty dollar over the lives of men and women like you, like me.   —DR. KWAME B. JOHNSON

It was 11:00 p.m. Bleary-eyed, Jennifer turned from the office wall clock, still elbow deep in editing *Unearthing Your Inner Ancestor*, the debut essay collection of Dr. Kwame B. Johnson—oft-quoted aca-demic, Black blogosphere sensation, and also the man whose home she had found herself skulking from in the wee hours that morn-ing. She was getting too old for this walk of shame shit. She was tired, good and tired. Yawning, she pushed back from a desk littered with pulp and type. The late hour had a feeling of finality, a signa-ture of the blood pact she had made for her promotion to senior editor at Onyx Ink—a fledgling imprint providing "a hip, new alternative for the discriminating reader of color." Or so claimed the sanguine memos of the international publishing giant that employed her. She yawned once more.

The day had been exhausting from the jump.

Howard Booker had practically been jumping out of his skin that morning.

"No, absolutely not, Mr. Booker," she repeated, for the fifth time during their meeting. Running late, Kwame's funk on her still, she sat listening in exasperation as the old man raged on. At her. At his own impotence. He was her publisher in name only, a man grandfathered in with the acquisition of his self-owned press so proudly "Black-owned, Black-operated for Forty-Three Years!" Or so claimed the rusted tin window sign of his now-shuttered Harlem shop.

"It's not just Antoine Deforest," she continued. "We're revisiting everyone's contracts. You, better than anyone, know how unmerciful this industry can be. Best seller or bust."

He grew blustery then. Leaning over her desk, his puffy gray Afro a sooty snowball hurtling toward her head. "Twenty-three years, young lady. Twenty-three years I've been printing that boy's books. He's family."

She stood then. Squared up.

"And that's exactly why we've kept him on this long," she said, "in spite of piss-poor book sales and, quite frankly, some pretty damn lackadaisical output on his part."

He turned from her, gazing out through the floor-to-ceiling windows.

"Twenty-three years," he muttered once more, his words deflated, a winded swan song. He was a proud one, a self-made man whose press, with its backlist of Afro-Caribbean treatises and Harlem Renaissance reprints, had fought the good fight, yet ultimately lost to street lit titles like *Pimps Need Love Too* and *A Hustler's Revenge: The Return of Makaveli Jesus*.

She backed down. She was sorry, but it was the job, *them's the breaks*, she told herself. Her new title, her *oh so substantial* salary, this shiny new office with its beveled-mirror Borghese desk—these all were markers that someday soon would come due. The higher-ups expected results: speedy and rocket-fueled. And yes, it had chafed at first, her role as hatchet woman for her own. She had risen through the publishing ranks on her own merit, championing and grooming a wide spectrum of emerging talents, then suddenly she was asked to head up an imprint, for—wink, wink—"her demographic." Cotton-picked to be their negro whisperer, their urban interlocutor. It was deeply irksome, but she adapted, did the good work she could, when she could. Trying to save more than she lost.

"Look, Mr. Booker, Howard," she began again, voice softer, tactful she hoped. "We can still push his ebooks. We can—"

"Twenty-three years," he said, for the final time, arms flapping upward toward the cloudless blue sky, somehow winged in his billowing dashiki as he turned away and took flight.

The clock read 11:30 p.m. now. Another yawn went smothered and palmed. If she hurried, she could finish the last chapter, finally on page 737 of all eight-hundred-odd pages of the manuscript. She would need to make substantial cuts; he did go on so, this man. He liked the sound of his own voice, but fortunately so did she, so ready she was to gamble, throw a hot hand of dice, that her readers would too.

Thumb bookmarking her page, she absently scratched a phantom braid that itched like the memory of a lost limb. The hairstyle had barely lasted a week, a brief seven-day countdown, before the Brillo-pad itch and scratch drove her back to the braid salon to perch on the lumpen leather of a swivel chair once again. The braider had harrumphed and tut-tutted her disapproval even as she clipped and unraveled each byzantine plait from Jennifer's head. Lanky Kanekalon extensions inched across linoleum floor tiles, like worms gone to ground.

Midnight, 12:00 a.m. It was a Wednesday. Kwame would be free to see her. She hurriedly wrapped up—logged off screens, replaced files—before resolutely shutting the office door behind her. That itch again. For his sake, she sometimes missed the braids. He had loved to twist them, fist them as he took her from behind. At times, she still felt the sting, that urgent tug at her temples, the quick snap of her neck backward as he took it all, had his way with her—his a hard way, one of gutters and gritty cries.

Locked

Jennifer's best friend would later deny it all, threaten to swear on a stack of Bibles, Torahs, Qur'ans, grimoires even—that she was innocent of the whole affair. Egobunma, best known as Ego, also known as Jennifer's bestie, brought Kwame into her life. She had strong-armed their crew into attending a "Get Up, Stand Up" reading series one Wednesday night, part of an ongoing campaign to transform their clique into social justice warriors (she was determined to single-handedly reclaim that title from those who hurled it insultingly). Only loyalty to their friend had pried Jennifer and Jada, her co-editor/work wife, from their desks and looming deadlines. They fully embraced the chance to support Ego's altruism. On the weekends. But this was an emergency. Ego was getting grief from her parents about her ill-paying nonprofit "work," their long-distance chagrin fulsomely expressed in weekly $3/minute phone diatribes from their hilltop Lagos estate. Their brilliant daughter was still unmarried, still "squandering" her Ivy League degree on do-gooding: a variety of projects on the continent. In February, she was relieving Third World debt; in August, eradicating FGM; this winter it was famine relief. "Adulting" was a bitch when you wanted to change the world.

So there they were, in a packed community college auditorium, hands daisy-chained as Ego tugged them forward, squeezing through the audience on a hunt for three empty seats side by side. There were none adjoined, so Jennifer landed on the aisle, next to an older Black woman who was such an avowed fan she'd snuck off work early and caught two buses to be there that night, she shared. She offered Jennifer half a corned beef sandwich, apologizing profusely for the smell of her delayed din-din, whipping out an unbruised Granny Smith apple from a Ziploc baggie in place of the first offering Jennifer declined.

Munching on apple, Jennifer scanned the program and its brief bio for a sense of this Kwame Johnson who had ladies playing hooky from their jobs to be there. Her first impression was not good. The program was already twenty minutes behind schedule and Jennifer wished she was back at the office. Reviewing manuscripts on her phone was a nonstarter and she'd already dispatched all her pending work emails. She looked at her friends, seated together, three rows back. Ego gave her a look of chagrin. Jada, ever the optimist, gave her two effusive thumbs-up, her trusty knitting needles in each hand, stabbing the air. Jennifer cackled at the disturbed look of the man to Jada's left who leaned away as if Jada had yelled "en garde." Classic Jada. She used any moment of downtime to stitch away and recently had started making whimsical cozies for her two ornate box turtles, Porgy and Bess.

The stage lights flickered and Jennifer's row mate whooped in excitement. "You going to love him."

Jennifer replied with a tepid smile as the lights dimmed. She waited.

It was his locks Jennifer had noticed first, coiled high atop his head like drowsy fattened cobras. Then the man spoke. And *oh mercy* and *my, my, my*, she was mesmerized, *fucking gobsmacked* by the play of muscle and mudcloth and spotlit brown skin. He strode across the stage. Fearsome and convicted, like some warrior-priest of old.

Something shook loose in Jennifer's throat, she swallowed, felt starved, ravenous.

Afterward, she shook loose from her trance, readied her business card and her spiel. Cut through the coterie of ankh-chained women who swarmed the author, clinging to him with worshipful eyes and the cloying stank of their patchouli.

"Jennifer Tchandep. Carbon House Publishing." She extended a gold-embossed card. "Give me a call and let's get you onto bookshelves."

Kwame scanned her face, then the card. "It says Onyx Ink."

"We're an imprint," she said, "catering to premier readers of color."

His smile, slow-coming, was sharp. "So they put you in charge of the publishing ghetto. Books for the 'Coloreds-Only' crowd."

Her fingers curled into a fist.

"Relax now, relax. I'm just playing with you, Queen." His second smile was high wattage, full of blinding, mind-numbing charm. "I respect the hustle. We'll talk."

She noted spitefully that his right canine was slightly longer than the left. At least there was that. But this was business so she collected herself, unfurled fists gone too tight, felt exiled blood light into her fingertips, here and there and here again, like frenzied fireflies, mating. Hands behind her back now, she rubbed and rubbed the rictus of her fingers, then willed them back to lie harmlessly at her sides.

She would someday recall that moment, could chart the evolution to her smaller, *hush now* self, to that woman who conceded all, every bit of her body his, down to the marbled skin of her very own teeth.

But this was the beginning so she flashed those pearlies. Smiled wide and somewhat true.

"You could say that," she answered him brightly. "Or you could say that our readers and writers need a room of their own. They need—"

"—affirmative action, the Black literati edition."

"—market share, the might and the power of numbers."

At that he went quiet. Money no laughing matter, this much she knew. She looked him over, took his measure, leaving the weight of her gaze on his bones, then took leave with one parting shot. "Call me, Dr. Johnson. Ask around, I'm very good."

They met for lunch at Joloff, a popular Senegalese restaurant in Brooklyn, and Kwame's favorite eatery according to a glowing profile—he's Ta-Nehisi Coates meets Marcus Garvey!—in the *New York Amsterdam News*. Though she was fifteen minutes early, Jennifer found him tableside, already seated and waiting.

"Right on time. Come, come," he said, beckoning her.

She walked over, stood by her chair a moment, which lapsed into another, expecting Kwame to stand. He took a long sip of his drink, a viscous, bloody concoction—*bissap*, she later learned. She seated herself.

A waiter approached the table with a menu in hand that Kwame waved away imperiously.

"She'll have the *tiebuu jeun*," he told the waiter, then to her, "Trust me. It's the only thing worth eating here, almost as good as the one I had in Dakar. You know, the restaurants downtown are whitewashed, more about candle lights and crisp linen than your meal. Joloff keeps it real. Authentic."

The waiter's face was placid, noncommittal. "Anything to drink? We have a superb house white."

"A glass of red," said Jennifer, her tone daring Kwame to order for her again. She was filled with irritation and a strange charge she had yet to identify.

"So, you think your book is going to free Black folk from mental slavery?" she asked.

"I think eating should always be a communal experience," he said, that right eyetooth of his flashing.

What in the world was this negro taking about? Jennifer thought. Now what she actually said was much more well measured, succinct. "How so?"

"Eating," he said, "is an act of nourishment. It's not about this spoon. It's about coming . . . together." He licked said spoon clean—neatly and thoroughly.

Lord.

"What it's about is tradition. About families gathered in a hut, sitting around one dish or one fire, telling their stories, eating as a whole, nourishing their souls. That's what the book is about. Nourishment. Are you hungry, Ms. Tchandep?"

She was ravenous.

The fish was fiery. Jennifer doused her flaming tongue with gulp after gulp of cool water, more than a tad bit peeved, as Kwame sat there oblivious, chewing with gusto, jaw movements so vigorous she thought it might unhinge. As a stray grain of rice fell to his lower lip, she practically sat on her hand to keep from brushing it away. Watched in fascination as that grain tumbled down below his waist, to parts unknown.

"A dream," she said hoarsely. She would, *dammit*, she could break through this ridiculous haze with pub industry chatter, with shop talk. "You're selling a dream, albeit a pretty tantalizing one. So we're all supposed to take a ride in this way-way-back machine, head to a simpler time, in some fantasy, virginal motherland."

"There are some things that should always be simple; some things that are elemental," he said. "Look, I'm not trying to be Malcolm or Martin. It's not up to me to lead. Our people were led onto slave ships and we followed, got Pied-Pipered right into bondage. So yeah, I've got a few things to say about agency and self-determination, about never being led that far astray again. Folks will or they won't move to action on their own."

"Sounds like a revolution," she said.

"Won't be televised," he said, smiling.

"Trust me," she said with spirit, surprising herself by her passion. "It'll be live at eleven. I can sell revolution. You say you want to reach people—well, that takes marketing, takes a team. Your message won't get out there as some dingy paperback on a collapsible table on the corner of 125th and nowhere."

He laughed softly at that.

Just then they heard the *adhan* of the corner mosque, the *muezzin* calling the faithful to worship, hailing true believers.

"I believe you," he said.

Twisted

The birthday party had been ablaze with candles. Not the anorexic, cake-topper variety—these were waxy and robust, thick with fragrance. Every surface was laden with their musk, mingling with aromas of honeydew, sugarcane, and sweets. Despite their cheerful flickers from every nook, the room somehow seemed shadowy to Jennifer. She twisted her hand in Kwame's, squeezed tighter.

It was their seventh date. If one could call a night honoring Yoruba deities at an Orisha ceremony in the bowels of Kwame's five-story apartment building a date. Jennifer had come to think of their outings together as cultural safaris as they hiked and trekked to all things African and Afrocentric in NYC. In the month since they'd first met, Kwame had taken her on a whirlwind tour of the locales featured in *Unearthing Your Inner Ancestor.* There had been a field trip to the Weeksville Heritage Center, a historical site marking the homestead of a pre–Civil War community of Black freedmen. They'd spent the day wandering among the whitewashed clapboards of people who had built a sanctuary out of nothing. Out of each other.

She would someday recall that visit, wondering how they conjured up the strength to rebuild it all, as she broke away from him, sought her own manumission.

But for now, there were other excursions: the African Burial Ground National Monument—largest colonial-era cemetery for people of African descent, a site in Foley Square she had flown by dozens of times—running errands, on her way to City Hall—yet had never truly taken notice of. She quietly admitted as much to Kwame as she read the inscriptions etched into the memorial wall, feeling Adinkra lettering ripple under her fingertips like runes.

"Sometimes it takes a bit of digging to *unearth the hidden ancestors* right in front of you," he said.

She turned, ready to tease him about "sappy book title wordplay that was only panty-dropping to his little groupies," but then she caught the edge of a look, one that made her wonder. *Did he, does he feel it too?*

He was all business after that, ever the gentleman, ever the dutiful tour guide. So she had shrugged it off, unsure what exactly she wanted or expected of him.

"What next?" she asked. "Where to?"

Next was holding hands in a candlelit room. He, grasping her hand to guide her through the throng. Their bodies jostled by dozens of whirling dervishes, dancing and chanting. A long-limbed woman swung past, moving in graceful parabolas that skimmed the press of bare feet and bare chests around the *trono* altar. Jennifer recognized her as Hanifah, whom Kwame had introduced earlier as his "spiritual

godmother." She had a head full of flowing two-strand twists that cas-
caded along her spine, glass beads and cowries caught in their wake like
dazzling flotsam.

"How is this a birthday party again?" Jennifer whispered to Kwame
during a break in the dancing.

"It's for Ade," he said, raising the arrow of their clasped hands to
point at a man standing at the head of the *trono* altar. "It's the anniversary of his initiation as a priest. His religious birthday."

"Ah," Jennifer said, wishing the birthday boy would blow out some
candles. The basement rec room was sweltering, separated from the
furnace inferno by a flimsy drywall partition. Sweat pooled in her col-
larbones. Her light muslin gown weighed heavily on her fevered skin,
yet she was loath to roll up her sleeves and risk violating some unspoken
rule for modesty of dress.

The sacred beats of the *bata* drums, and the warm rumble of Kwame's
murmured explanations on their meanings, were a welcome distraction. The three drummers sat serenely, colorful cloths across their laps
swaddling *iya*, the mother drum; *itotele*, the middle drum; and the little
brother drum, *okonkolo*, he told her.

"The drums are consecrated, created to talk to the gods," said Kwame.
"Their three voices combined sound like Yoruba, mimicking its tones
and inflections."

He spoke softly into the coil of her ear, his fingertips tapping her hip
in time with the drums.

"They are cajoling." Tap, tap. "Pleading." Tap-tap, tap-tap. "Begging
Yemaya to please, please leave her heavenly home in *orun*, come join
us here on *aiye*."

There was a frenzy then. A quickened tempo. Ade, the priest, strut-
ted forward, head jutting like a preening cock's, downing sweaty swigs
from a bottle of gin before spraying the mouthful over the drummers.
Drunk with heat, Jennifer swayed away unsteadily, felt stray droplets
rain down on her, stumbled as the group pushed in to receive their
libations, their blessings. She scrambled backward, retreated farther,
stopping short to look down in horror, gasping at the sight of her left

foot planted squarely, blasphemously, on the sacred mat in front of the altar—off-limits to the uninitiated and initiated alike. She jerked away, eyes darting up to search for witnesses, for accusers, but instead found Kwame, his large frame moving toward her, scything through bodies with grim determination. The *pam-pam-tak-tat-tak* of drumbeats punched through her thoughts, *tam-tamming* a secret alarm, a warning to *flee now, sister, flee*. She was so hot, so frantic in her need for a door, an open window, for air, a place to breathe. And still the drums pounded harder and faster, her heart thumping in sync, a crazed counterrhythm, a primal call-and-response, skipping altogether as she was wrenched from behind, tumbling backward into the dark, scream muffled by a surge of voices all around her, devotees singing out:

Iyá eyá ayaba okun omá iré gbogbo awani Iyá

She smelled frankincense and saltwater, felt a warm hand holding a cool glass of water to her lips. *Hanifah.* "Drink, little sister. You looked like you were about to pass out."

Seated on a low wooden bench, Hanifah plied Jennifer with water, fed her sugarcane from the altar, kissed her forehead, her cheeks, smiling gently, somehow satisfied by what she felt there. Jennifer closed her eyes, slow inhales and ponderous exhales rocking the cradle of her rib cage. Soothed, she drifted off a few moments, maybe more, before she felt Hanifah's warm hands on her own, pulling her up again, pulling her deep into the dance. She rose up, hips moving hesitantly at first, footsteps plodding, overly cautious, but soon a slow urgency overcame her, seeped into her bloodstream with the swell of the music, and then she was dancing, with abandon, with uncut joy. Hanifah embraced her again, spinning their bodies round and round, before presenting Jennifer back to Kwame with a flourish. His arms wide open, waiting to enfold her.

"Yemaya has blessed you," he said. "It's a great honor . . . not every guest gets invited to dance with the Orishas."

"*Ase o*," she replied, rolling her hips backward, beginning the dance anew.

What seemed like hours later, an overhead light flickered on, and Jennifer blinked below its sudden glare like some night thing accustomed to darkness always.

"What next?" she asked Kwame, climbing up from the well of her daze, body supple and radiant with sweat.

"Nourishment," he said, a stalk of sugarcane grasped in his fist like a spear. "We'll make a feast of offerings for the gods."

He peeled back the rough skin of the cane with sharp teeth, sucked deeply before pressing it into her hands.

"Eat," he murmured.

She licked its juices appreciatively, the sweet giggle of sap meeting the salty bite of her sweat. She licked again, then held up the stalk and its sticky meat to him.

"Delicious," he said. His head bowed now, somehow solemn, as he leaned in close to take everything she was offering.

Pressed

When Jennifer was a child, her mother had pressed her kinks with a hot comb each Saturday night. By Sunday morning she was pew-bound, hair as prim and starch-straight as the pleats of her somber navy skirt. When she was bright-eyed and Sunday-schooled, Jennifer saw her obedience as Christlike, saw the lick of holy fire in the blue flames of the oven range. Grew to welcome—hands meekly folded in her lap—the molten hot comb as God's shining instrument. It was about enduring, a test and a testimony. She never squirmed, though her mind filled with premonitions of hellfire during the brimstone sizzling of her strands. Still, there were signs and wonders to be had in the steadiness of her mother's hand. She was never burned. Bore no errant mark of Cain. Her mother was faithful to this evening ritual, these kitchen vespers. God forbid the Rapture came and her child was found nappy and wanting.

As a young woman, Jennifer, much like her hair, grew unruly—roamed free and unfettered, nights wild and her own. This was how she felt now on the Saturdays that Kwame came to her demanding many things—both monstrous and delightful. She learned to relish Sunday morning's bruises and welts as signs and wonders of their sweet tussle. Knowing she had likewise marked him with tooth and nail and the slick of her tongue. Only with him did she discover her appetites. How she liked the rough mouthful that was the word *fuck* on her tongue almost as much as the thing itself. Liked to trace her toe along the seam of him just to watch him grow shivery—becoming a herky-jerky creature, a thing unspooled.

After he had gone, back to parts unknown, she would lie there short of breath, yet finally, fully alive, her face pressed to the sheets to catch remnants of his smell—a smoky, spicy thing that brought to mind foreign altars where the righteous sacrificed loved ones to their insatiable gods.

Blowout

He kept her in bed for days at a time. Sweating out her blowout. Edges and toes curling again and again. In moments between, she would lie along the stalk of him. Tracing twin scars along the hollow of his side. *Battle wounds*, he'd answered to questions unspoken. Ear to chest. Hairs tickling her cheek. His voice a grumbling lullaby telling tales of ancestors: of kings, of queens from Africa past. He claimed them by birthright. No genealogy sites traced his DNA across the diaspora. Yet by his estimate, he was descended from Sheba and Sundiata, from Makeda and Menelik. He joked about his credentials—a Morehouse, Princeton, and Harvard alum. Bread-and-buttered on the stoops of Bed-Stuy, where your street cred—the only pedigree that truly mattered—was measured by number of shots survived, by who and how many feared you.

He was cocky. Completely at ease in his skin and his identity. It was seductive as fuck. Head on his chest, Jennifer sometimes bit down on his nipple till she drew blood: craving him, suckling in that knowing ease for herself. She, the child of a timid mother, ever grateful for kitchen scraps. One of two Black girls in Scarsdale elementary class portraits, backdropped against classmates with skin the color of flash paper, burning memories of her away. Her mother had stayed mute on the subject of their culture. What did she know of her heritage? Her brilliant ancestry. No matter how many boardroom doors Jennifer walked through, sometimes she felt her steps falter—in the Ghanaian beauty shop, at Awing tribal meetings, she felt like a counterfeit African, felt the unworthiness of the maid's child tiptoeing through the servants' entrance, lightly, quietly, like she was walking on cowrie shells.

"You're already African. Period. Point blank. That man is brainwashing you." Ego—natural-hair guru, early convert to the cult of the "Big Chop"—was at her condo greasing her scalp, offering up unsolicited wisdom on maintaining a 4C TWA and your sense of self.

"Ow," Jennifer cried, kneeling bedside, head bent in unwilling supplication to her friend's ministrations. "Could you scratch any harder? I think you got some brain with that."

"Stop with the whining," Ego said, scraping toothy comb to scalp. "It's not my fault you're so tender-headed. Blame your addiction to creamy crack. You know all those chemicals leach right into your skin, right?"

"Okay, enough," Jennifer said, breaking free from the tangle of Ego's knees. "I've got like zero time for your anti-perm PSA today. I've still got to beat my face, do my nails, iron my dress—"

"Okay, okay. Calm down, Ms. Lady," said Ego. "All you need is a light touch-up. I've got some press-ons in my bag if you're pressed for time. And I'll iron the dress. Is it that little *kente* confection over there?" Her comb pointed accusingly at the offending garment, hanging boldly on the front of Jennifer's closet door. "Who bought that? Your mother. No. Of course not. It's from *him*. Girl, if you read that *So Afrique* blog piece I sent you, you'd know better than to put up with this five-percenter bullshit. My girl Lapis knows what's up."

"I read one," Jennifer said, chuckling softly. The article was a pan-

African ranking of men from all corners of the continent—from Naija and Camer to Zim—rated on everything from ding-a-ling size to level of "wokeness" on gender roles. "She's funny."

"She's the truth. You need to learn something. That man's got you twisted. Doubting everything about yourself. Mr. Back-to-Africa, High Priest of Hotep is what he really is."

"I told you not to call him that." Jennifer met Kwame's watchful eyes in the framed photo at her bedside. Ego had barreled over from her next-door apartment so quickly she hadn't had a chance to tuck it away in the top drawer, a knee-jerk reaction, she realized, so accustomed she was to hiding evidence of their relationship from her colleagues at work.

"Pass me that iron," Ego said, sticking out a hand. "And I'll call him what I like. He gave you a name."

"It's just a pet name," Jennifer countered, grabbing her makeup and a mirror.

"Whatever you say, *Jumanji*," Ego replied, then said "ow," singeing a finger as she tested the heat of the iron.

"See, that's what you get," said Jennifer. "God don't like ugly. And the name is Jamila. It's Arabic for 'beautiful.'"

When they met, Kwame had been surprised by her lack of a traditional "country" name. But he had yet to meet her mother. Innocent Tchandep had come to America thirty years prior as a domestic live-in for the Cameroonian ambassador. She had been grateful, very grateful, to the ambassador, a man from her village. After all, cleaning a mansion was better than cleaning a hut. Ultimately, her expressions of gratitude had resulted in a pregnancy and an invective-filled discharge by the ambassador's wife. But her mother had still been grateful to be in the land of opportunity and began her lifelong quest to guarantee said opportunities for her daughter by giving her newborn the only gift she could afford at the time, a marker for access and entitlement: the blondest of all-American names—Jennifer.

"Anyway. You're one to talk. I thought you were into the whole African renaming thing," said Jennifer, darkening her smoky eye.

Ego snorted, a weak rebuttal given her proclivity for boyfriends named after dead African presidents. In the past year alone, there had been a Nkrumah, a Lumumba, and a Kenyatta né Michael, Douglas, and Romeo, respectively.

Jennifer scratched the base of her hair where tiny fire ants still danced a devilish jig. She was going to be late.

"Stop that. You'll get grease all over that dress of yours." Ego rummaged through her worn *ukara* cloth bag of potions and tricks, triumphantly producing a jar of the tea tree oil concoction she swore by. "Move your hand and let me rub this in," she offered softly, her hands moving through Jennifer's hair. "It's not about the name. It's about you feeling like who you are isn't good enough, not African enough. You don't have to jump through all these cultural hoops and hair loop-de-loops for some man you just met. I love you just as you are."

Jennifer felt something inside her chest shift. She laughed to shake it loose.

"Ego. You change your hair like every other day! Folks can barely recognize you half the time. And Kwame's not telling me to do a damn thing. My hair, my choices."

Feeling Ego's hands stilled in her hair, she turned her neck to look her friend in the eye, hoping to convince her, to convince them both.

"If you say so," said Ego, her own eyes doubtful, even as she answered her friend's silent plea to change the subject. "What's all this dress-up for again and how come I wasn't invited?"

"It's an NAACP fund-raiser and I slid an invite under your door a week ago."

"Oh."

"Yeah. 'Oh.' *Anyways*, I'll see you this Friday night for the Kwanzaa celebration," she said. "And don't even think about canceling on us again. He's really looking forward to meeting you."

"I'll try . . . you know I've been swamped with work this month."

"Work." Jennifer suppressed a snort of her own.

"Is your man reading from his book?" Ego's voice was conciliatory.

"More publicity, more money," said Jennifer, ready to make peace herself. She pulled her friend close, loosely hugging her about the waist as they looked at their twinned reflections in the bedroom mirror: Jennifer, Ovaltine-colored; Ego, a bittersweet dark chocolate. This woman was an extension of her, her opinion prized. She bent her head to lay it down on Ego's shoulder, then spoke to their mirrored selves, "You better come through on Friday. Staying at home, eating Jiffy Pop, and watching hipster porn is not an option."

She watched Ego's reflection smile back at her. Ego—admittedly "sooo exhausted by the New York meat market"—was becoming a bit of a recluse. Indoors most nights. Getting her kicks from feminist porn—ethical smut starring consenting, well-paid performers with ironic body hair—Xander in muttonchops with chest whiskers peeking up from the V of his flannel work shirt—or Fantasia with Bettie Page bangs and a furry vulva carved in the shape of Cupid's bow, pointing to pleasure. A simple formula, really: lumbersexual boy meets hipster girl. The course of XXX celluloid love forever running smooth. No complications. No kinks.

Wrapped

It was Friday night, December 31, and a *karamu* feast celebrating the end of Kwanzaa was well under way when Jennifer arrived at the strange door. She stood there filled with uncertainty, wishing Kwame had picked her up as he had promised. Quelling the urge to tiptoe over yet another threshold, she squared her shoulders and knocked. The door swung inward of its own accord, the sound of ululating and *djembe* drumming greeted her. Kwame did not. Even though she had texted him that she was right outside.

Two steps into the hallway, a burly man accosted her with a "Free Mumia" flyer and literature on the "Rebirth of the Five Percenter." She pushed past him into a thicket of damp bodies, lightly perspiring in their voluminous caftans. She straightened the hem of her beige Maison Margiela jacket, then chuckled at her own silliness. No *kente* dresses for her today. Running late from work, she had barely had enough time to pick up a *zawadi* from the boutique near her office. *Zawadi*. That was what the colorfully wrapped Kwanzaa gifts were called. A recently learned factoid come courtesy of a giraffe in a skirt. Earlier that day, she had confessed ignorance about the details of the holiday to Jada, ending in a three-part defense: (a) I grew up in Scarsdale, (b) I went to Yale, (c) my mother is Cameroonian. There is no Kwanzaa in Africa. It's a holiday created for people whose culture was stolen from them.

Later in the day, a selection from their children's book division came to her interoffice: *Kiana's First Kwanzaa*, a gold seal certifying it as a Coretta Scott King Award winner. The Kiana in question was a young giraffe girl who taught her that *umoja* meant "unity," that the candelabra on the table in front of her was a *kinara*, and that its seven candles represented the seven principles of Kwanzaa. There was something else she tried to remember about fertility and corn, but thoughts of that fled as she spotted Kwame in a corner chair, with a white woman draped across his lap.

There was a tap on her shoulder, a *Hey girl*. She turned her head, a brusque *I'm here with someone* on her lips, but it was only Ego. Swiveling back to look across the room, she saw the woman was now leaning on the wall beside Kwame's chair. Ego pulled at her arm.

"You're late," Jennifer said.

"I know," said Ego, eyes narrowed, as she peered across the room. "Let's go say hi to those two. That corner looks cozy."

They walked over together, arm in arm.

Up close the woman was emaciated, near to toppling under the weight of a towering head wrap. This Becky in Badu drag symbolized everything Kwame despised, or so she had believed on those nights kneeling at his knee, a rapt pupil, attentive as he prepared the next school day's lecture on issues of "cultural appropriation" and "critical race theory." Who was this man? Who was this woman? Had Kwame been *learning* her too? Had he taught her to mind him, to want, no, to *revel* in the pleasure of his yoke? She searched his face for answers. His expression held none.

"*Hotep*, my sisters," said Kwame's sloe-eyed companion, sizing up Jennifer and Ego before wisely walking off.

"Hello," said Jennifer, then to Kwame, still seated, "hello to you too." He stood. Hugged her. Then moved to do the same with Ego, who bobbed and weaved away from his embrace.

He folded in on himself, empty arms hugging his own chest. "You ladies enjoying the festivities?"

"It's an interesting holiday," said Ego. "Swahili lingo and a candelabra that's two sticks short of a menorah. Oy vey." She rolled her eyes and looked at Jennifer, who knew she was just saying this to piss off Kwame. Sometimes her friend was the bitch Jennifer wished she could be.

"Jamila, I think your friend is missing the point," said Kwame. "She'll come around. For now, let's get you ladies some drinks." He turned and walked off. His signature method for conflict avoidance, one Jennifer had become all too familiar with of late. Infuriating. And probably the reason he'd been stabbed by no less than three ex-girlfriends. *Battle wounds, my ass. Serves him right.* And not for the first time she wondered what she'd be pushed to, what it would take to truly reach this man. She felt herself moving to follow him instinctively nonetheless. She was pulled backward by another tug on her arm, then Ego's voice asking, "Who are you?"

"I don't have time for this," she said.

"I'm sorry. Are we in a hurry to go walk five steps behind your man?"

"Why did you have to antagonize him?"

"I don't like him."

"You barely know him."

"No. You're the one who's acting brand-new. Him, I've known for weeks now," Ego insisted. "I've seen him through you. Watched him morph you into some tragic cultural mulatto. Kwame tells you to get braids so you get calluses on your butt sitting for twelve hours, for some treetops-of-the-Serengeti hairstyle you scratch out your head in two days. He tells you what 'authentic' dishes to cook, when he'll come over to eat them, what 'culturally imperialist' Western music not to listen to. And you do it. You do it all."

"You're full of shit," said Jennifer, filled with an anger she only dimly registered was displaced. "You just want me to be unhappy like you and your dead prezzes."

"At least I know what I'm getting with them. Kwame is such a phony. He's a tyrant in bougie, enlightened-brother clothing."

It was Ego's turn to leave her then.

Rooted in place, Jennifer let the drumming, the ululating, the press of bodies push into and over her; felt waves of fury, doubt, and humiliation—shot through with love, still and always love. The man she loved hadn't noticed, said nothing, *nothing* about her other *zawadi* for him, a surprise, a coronation, her crown freshly garlanded by soft and springy sisterlocks.

Shorn

It would be weeks before she left him. Longer still for his own farewell. She cooked him a last supper on one of their final nights together. Unaware of endings when she woke that morning for a bright and early pilgrimage to the market, purchasing the freshest of fish for their six-month anniversary dinner. There were no premonitions as she warmed palm oil, diced onions, sliced carrots. She hummed as she chopped Scotch bonnet peppers and wild turnips and sweet cassava and bruise-colored eggplants. She stirred and simmered. She boiled. The sauce bubbled, filling her kitchen with the tender scent of hibiscus flowers and tamarind. In her nostrils, in her hair.

That night, she lay crisp white linen on the table. When he came to her, she served him, uncovered the dish before him, waiting. For what? Praise? Vindication? This is how her mother must have served the ambassador, she imagined, hovering eagerly, so hopeful in her fawning, even as his wife sat watchful, ever watchful, at the far end of the dinner table.

Jennifer recalled herself, fixed her own plate, sat watchful as Kwame pushed his dish away. She waited for an explanation, for a request to pass the salt or Maggi or hot sauce. Instead he took slow, excruciating sips from his glass of water.

"Eat," she told him finally, leaning forward, scooping a fine-boned piece of fish to his lips. An offering. "Eat."

This time, it was her hand he pushed away. "I'm not hungry," he said. The sound of those words a tumbleweed of thorny hurts and rough disappointments rolling through her apartment, gathering and growing, till finally she spoke.

"Nourishment," she said, echoing the words of a man she had once thought so wise.

"What?"

"Nourishment, remember? Tradition. You and me, together, sitting around one dish. Eating what I spent the whole damn day preparing. You've been asking for this meal for weeks. Been saying how much you wanted some homemade *tiebuu jeun*, a home-cooked African meal."

"But it's not . . . you're not really *African* African, are you?"

What was she then? she wondered. *What did he see when he looked at her?*

He stood behind her now, kneading her shoulders, pushing pliancy into her flesh, saying, "Jamila, don't be so sensitive. You know what I meant. I've traveled and lived across the motherland. So you tried your hand at making a Senegalese dish. No harm in it, but you're not Senegalese, right? I mean, sometimes I feel like you're barely even Cam—"

She pulled away from him then, aching to aim a fist at that flashing eyetooth, leave him gumming his words, their bite stolen. *How could he say such things?* He sounded so self-assured, so decided, like he had sussed out the mystery of her just by sampling the salt of her moans. But if she thought hard on it, traced the true shape of his thoughts, his patterns, this man thought he had the measure of most things really, so why would something as simple as a woman be unknowable to him?

And then, a turn, a change of tactics. This is where he kissed her bare shoulder, the petal blade of her collarbone. A quizzical slant to his jaw, as Jennifer, become fluent in the lexicon of his body, its tenses and full stops, read all. Fingers pinching pressure points along the bridge of his nose, signaling exasperation, demanding: *Why, really why would she make him teach her such hard truths about herself, make him repeat the obvious?* Squared shoulders bulged like boulders, resolute, soldiering on because *hadn't he taught her much, he, the authority that they both knew he was, vetted and credentialed, soon-to-be published author of a book on this very subject.* Brisk shake of the head—in resignation? in acknowledgment?—that *he'd done his part, had he not? He'd taught others, so many others whose flush-faced ignorance was infuriating, and still others sclerotic with misconceptions, but they had learned, he had prevailed.* And now that numbing, spirit-deadening smile of his as he saw a finish line beyond her. Because this was the moment in their arguments where she inevitably acquiesced, *the* moment, only briefly delayed, that her acceptance would come, made all the sweeter for the wait. In this moment, smugness draped on him like a plush robe, he was utterly himself. He was who he had ever been, she'd just been deaf and dumb to it.

When Jennifer was a little girl, carefree, swinging barefoot from sycamore trees, her mother had seen darkness on the horizon and offered protection, rubbed salves of cinnamon and almond oil on her skin, safeguarding a daughter whose blood was too sweet, one who always came home bitten over and over. Jennifer had been immaculate in her oblivion, until a day or so later she would look down in surprise to see pinched and angry flesh, bright shining evidence of her violation. Then and only then was she stung, floodgates of pain and irritation flung open.

This is how she felt now. Stung. Pain freshly exposed, made flesh.

She snatched up Kwame's plate, marching to the kitchenette, scraped and scraped its heaping helpings into the maw of the sink drain, then switched on the disposal. Its grating sputter and hacksaw grind were the only sound in the room.

He sidled up to her, looming large in the small kitchenette.

"Do you want me to leave, Jamila?"

She let the drone of the drain and running, fleeing water drown out his words, wishing that she could put all of it, all this mess, down this crunching void. What could be severed? What damaged parts, what hidden organs—her spleen, the pulp of her womb—localized whatever made her weak for him? Had it spread too far, oozed and metastasized to every mighty and insignificant bit of her? To the very fingers—knuckles to nailbeds—now hovering over this steel sinkhole?

Kwame's lips moved, his voice underscored by wailing in her head, by ringing in her ears. He switched off the deafening roar. "Did you hear me, Jamila? Jamila."

Her hands dropped to the lip of the sink. She raised them again, let the waterfall on tap cleanse the food scraps, took her time lathering and rinsing and drying, before finally turning to look him in the face full on. She took his hands in her clean ones, brought his hands to her face, let their palms cup her cheeks, let what she needed to tell him vibrate through the air and flesh. "Kwame Lucius Johnson. The name is Jennifer. Say my name, Jennifer."

In a different tale this would have been the end. She would claim her name and herself and that would be that. But this was her love story and she was a tenacious overachiever, willing to adapt, to try and try once more, so nothing happened of a sudden. She wrote pro and con lists on why to stay, why she should leave. Considered every what-if and maybe and someday till one day the exhaustion of it all overtook her. The man and his book were out and about in the world, away on multicity tours, the work they had done together bigger than her, bigger than him. Writ large on best-seller lists. With professional pride, she watched him proselytizing on late-night talk shows, held her breath at his words, found her mirror image in others as cameras panned to studio audiences, their eyes so open, so ready to trust and perhaps obey. She let herself breathe, one wobbly breath after another.

Other steps were harder, of course. A talk, a fight, a break. Yet real endings take a long time so for weeks he loomed large in her memories. A Leviathan. He lingered on street corners, on stoop fronts, at subway exits. She saw him everywhere. Walking the sunbaked streets of Harlem became a study in avoidance, a spiteful child's game as she hopscotched across hot sidewalks, each time she saw him in the curve of a stranger's jaw. Even then, her thoughts would skitter, stop at crosswalks to stand and wonder.

Soon she saw the signs, a pattern emerging. He was where his peculiar brand of Africanness was. So she excised it like a vestigial organ. But then, a reclamation, a defining of Africanness for herself as she and Ego took bold steps among the aisles of that African food mart, where she had bought his favorite goat meat. Chose filigreed fabrics and bright threads for an outfit by Abdullah, the Senegalese tailor who had promised, *insha'Allah*, to embroider wedding robes for her and Kwame.

Months passed. A millennium. Her locks hung long, loosed down her back. The day came when she could spool them. Coil them high atop her head. It was then she took his razor. Felt it—whetstone sharp and ready. Held flush against soft skin. A cut, a slash, a cut again. Fattened cobras on the floor. *Korobo* now. Her hands gliding across liberated skin. Stung by the sheer pleasure of it all.

Scan to read SoAfrique blog.

Acknowledgments

Imagining this book in the hands of the people who nourished my creativity on the page, even before I fully embraced it myself, is profoundly meaningful.

My wholehearted thanks go out to the many institutions who granted me the gift of unfettered days, space to commune with kindred spirits, and oftentimes three yummy hots and goose-down cots. Many thanks to the administrators, staff, founders at Kimbilio, Ucross, the MacDowell Colony, Vermont Studio Center, Stadler Center for Poetry at Bucknell University, Byrdcliffe Colony, Wurlitzer Foundation, Virginia Center for the Creative Arts, Clarion West Writers Workshop, and the Hub City Writers Project.

Thank you to the AKO Caine Prize, in particular Dele Fatunla, for giving writers from the continent the glow-up and uplift they more than deserve. Africa is not a country and we've still got a world of stories to tell.

To my hardworking editor, Steve Woodward, your keen eye for language and generous spirit made me truly feel seen. Thank you for the laughter and for bearing with my nitpicky, writerly ways. A galaxy of thanks to Fiona McCrae and everyone on the Graywolf team for my enthusiastic welcome into your wolfpack. Let's howl into the wind and be fierce together.

To my steadfast agent Rachel Kim at 3 Arts, your vision for my work and its possibilities is truly appreciated. When they're etching books directly onto retinas in some future world, I know you'll sell my eye-rights for millions.

My sincerest thanks to all the teachers who have encouraged me as a writer throughout the years: from that bluestocking of a girl reading Austen and writing Star Wars fan-fics to the writer of this very book, you saw value in my voice. Special thank-yous to Karen Russell, Sam Chang, Kevin Brockmeier, Kate Christiansen, Ethan Canin, Andrew Sean Greer, Lee K. Abbott, Cory Doctorow, Nalo Hopkinson, Susan Palwick, Toby Buckell, Andy Duncan, and Eileen Gunn.

Another rip-roaring thanks to Karen Russell, my dolphin sister, trans-mitting to me on those higher octaves. Thank you for being a friend/mentor/cheerleader who has loved on my work even in the rough. You read this manuscript time and time again and instinctively knew where I was trying to go even when I lost my footing. You are a gift, K-lista.

To Kevin Brockmeier once more, for your *Fraggle Rock*–loving weird and wonderful ways, for bringing tin robots and the *Codex Seraphinianus* into my life, and the many, many rec letters, thank you, thank you, thank you. And I still think you're an elven lord in disguise.

To Deb West, Connie Brothers, and Jan Zenisek, for your pat-ented method of making all paths smooth that seemed so rocky just moments prior, many thanks. Now tell me your secrets.

To every workshop-mate who has touched these pages and given of your time to make them better, thank you. Special shoutout to my homies from the days in them cornfield streets, they'll be handwritten inscriptions galore on your copies thanking you for editing, home-baked goods, photo shoot collabs, putting up shelves, and more. For now, just know this work IS because you are Christa Fraser, Clare Jones, Matthew Nelson Teutsch, Yaa Gyasi, Alexia Arthurs, Catina Bacote, Sarah Smith, Meredith Blankenship, Ryan Tucker, Shea Lynn Sadulski, Jennifer Percy, Derek Nnuro, Novuyo Rosa Tshuma, Kyle Minor, Tom Quach, and Naomi Jackson.

To the Clarion 2015 crew: Huw Evans (for encouraging me to write where the joy is), Neile Graham (for sci-fi poems and delicious scotch), and all my fellow nerdren writers who proudly wear a T-shirt emblazoned with the immortal words "I Like Stories Where All the Men Are Dead," thank you Christine Neulieb, Rebecca Campbell, Margaret Killjoy, Julia Wetherell, Evan Peterson, Samuel Kolawole, Laurie Penny, Mike Sebastian, Leo Vladimirsky, Justin Key, Tegan Moore, Nibedita Sen, Dinesh Pulandram, Jake Stone, Garrett Johnston, Thersa Matsuura, and Mimi Mondial.

To the wonderfully inquisitive students I have had the honor of teaching at the University of Alabama, the University of Iowa, and Coe College as well as the incredibly supportive faculty and staff therein, particularly Dr. Gina Hausknecht, unfailing writer of many a recommendation letter and warm intellect, you all challenged me to be my best.

To all my fellow travelers and friends along this circuitous path: Dr. Jacky Amadu Kaba, Malik Vassel, Lilian Oben, Lorraine Oben, Davis Enloe, Tigi Kanu, Christopher Hundley, Khary Russell, Rachelle Taylor, Felicity Tsikiwa, Idongesit Daniel, Rachel Achebodt, Catherine Essoka, Edinam Oton and the AFRican magazine fam, Bob and Lajuana Carabasi, the Ngangmuta familia: Aunty Hilda, Ngam, Ngong, Tosam, and Fulei—all the thanks in the universe.

Heartfelt thanks to my dearest friends, Sheryl Byfield, Chae Sweet, and Abosede George, who have been through the fire with me hand in hand. We're gilded and glorious now.

To the best road dogs a gal could have hoped for on this journey called life: Andzifor Kaba, smarty-pants, modelesque mother of giants, you are more than you know; Dr. Fongalla Ngoche Nkweti, chief by name, dopest conversationalist and old soul; Numbisi Loweh Nkweti, brightest star, effortless fashionista, and provoker of belly laughs, thank you all for your tireless, "by any means necessary" support: butt-kicking, pep talks, epic burns—you got the job done. I love you all on a cellular level. Dynasty time.

To all my kinfolk in the Nkweti clan, especially Clemence "Mother Teresa" Onana, Grace and Afo Ngu-Mbi and in the Nana bloodline, particularly Dr. Nana Jack Mofor, Stanley and Cecelia Withers, my deepest thanks for your prayers, for *koki* corn and *achu*, for raising me up to be the woman I am.

To God Almighty and all my ancestors in the afterlife, this work is pouring one out for you in words.

Illustration Credits

"Subway Katana." Credit: Rossowinch Art.

Jungle Jitters film still, Warner Bros., 1943. Used under public domain.

"If It Bleeds, It Ledes," and "Africa Is Not a Country." Credit: Idongesit Daniel.

"Shaka Zulu Queen Mother," January 1999. Copyright © Joshua Sinclair. Reproduced courtesy of the artist, Ouarzazate, Morocco.

In Memoriam

This is a tribute to my friend, "High Poetess" Paula Pryce Bremmer—beloved wife and mother, inspirational counselor to legions of students finding their way, and a gifted writer whose creative voice was snatched away from this world all too soon. She is one of so many souls senselessly lost to the pandemic. She made her mark on many hearts. She is loved.

Author's Note

Portions of this work cite real criminal cases, bearing witness to stories of trauma and lessons that should not be forgotten.

Nana Nkweti is a Cameroonian American writer, AKO Caine Prize finalist, and alumna of the Iowa Writers' Workshop. Her work has garnered numerous fellowships, from the MacDowell Colony, Kimbilio, Ucross, and the Wurlitzer Foundation, among others. As a professor of English at the University of Alabama, she teaches courses that explore her eclectic literary interests ranging from graphic novels to medical humanities on to Afrofuturism.

The text of *Walking on Cowrie Shells* is set
in Adobe Garamond Pro.
Book design by Rachel Holscher.
Composition by Bookmobile Design and Digital
Publisher Services, Minneapolis, Minnesota.
Manufactured by Versa Press on acid-free,
30 percent postconsumer wastepaper.